Abdul and the Designer Tennis Shoes

by William McDaniels

African American Images
Chicago, Illinois

Illustrations by Buck Brown

First Edition

Copyright © 1990 by William McDaniels

ABDUL AND THE DESIGNER TENNIS SHOES

Chapter One

Abdul slowly raised his head and turned over onto his side. Then he looked down at his feet. Spread over this 6'7" distance were one week's worth of socks in various colors, a jacket, some cassette tapes and a pair of "Long John's". After a few minutes, he stretched and then yawned, to clear what felt like thick cobwebs from his throat.

Finally he sat up motionless, with his head bent and his knees jutting out like two poles. He looked back at the small clock on the desk to the northwest of his bed. It was 6:30 a.m. Through the window to the left, he could see the sun rising, as it poured its light into the room, and onto the black and white poster of Michael Jordan, hanging on the wall before him. Jordan was doing one of his classic slam dunks.

Abdul stared at the poster with sleepy eyes, imagining himself soaring through the air like Jordan. Suddenly his mother's voice snapped him back to reality. "Get up and get dressed! Hurry up or you'll be late for school again," she yelled.

Abdul crawled out of the bed, and pulled on his sweater and jeans. Then he made his way down the stairs toward the kitchen. As he descended the stairs, the smell of frying bacon finally awakened him. His appetite began to swell as he walked into the kitchen. He met his mother at the stove, turning over one strip of bacon after another in a large black frying pan. He watched her as she frowned and poked the bacon with a long-handled fork.

She flinched as the hot grease and bacon crackled. She was wearing her "NUMBER ONE MOM" apron, a birthday present Abdul had given her. She smiled warmly as Abdul walked in. "Good morning, Son," she said.

"Morning," Abdul said with his eyes on the steaming pancakes, creamy eggs, and crisp bacon she was putting on his plate.

His brother Sonny was already slurping down his pancakes, with milk. By the time that Abdul sat next to him at the table, Sonny had a white milk mustache above his upper lip. He looked up at Abdul with mischief in his eyes and gave Abdul a long face. Abdul reached over to rub his head. Mischievously, Sonny cried out, "Mamma, Abdul hit me!"

Abdul's mother gave Abdul the evil eye. "Leave him alone and eat your breakfast," she warned.

"I didn't hit him, Mamma. He's lying."

"I'm not lying," Sonny said, proudly wiping the milk from his mouth with the back of his hand.

"You act like a baby, chump," Abdul said.

Before Sonny could answer, his mother gave them the evil eye again. "Abdul, instead of teasing him all of the time, why don't you try teaching your little brother some things for a change," she finally said.

"I try to, Mamma, but he won't listen! His head's as hard as this table," Abdul said, rapping his knuckles against the top of the table.

"His head is no harder than yours," his mother responded. "I've been telling you to clean your room all week. Now I want it cleaned before you leave for school. Do you hear me?"

"Yes, Ma'am," Abdul shrugged.

Abdul finished eating and hurried upstairs to his room. He stood in the middle of his room and looked around at his scattered clothes and messy bed. "Why does it have to be clean?" he thought. "No one ever uses it but me!"

First he made the bed. Then he started picking up the clothes that were scattered all over the room. For a moment he considered hanging them up. Then he changed his mind. Instead, he quickly stuffed them into the dresser drawer near the window. Feeling a little guilt, he glanced over his shoulder and through the doorway. When he was certain that his mother wasn't watching, he kicked a pair of shoes under the bed. Then, after checking to be sure that the room looked like everything was in place, he ran out of the room and headed down the stairs.

When he reached the bottom of the stairs, he saw that his mother was still in the kitchen. She was sitting at the table drinking coffee, and reading the morning newspaper. "I see you've got a game this week," she said.

"Yeah, what's the paper say?" Abdul asked, looking over his mother's shoulder, and giving her a quick hug.

"Nothing about you," Sonny teased, grinning and walking into the kitchen. Abdul started to respond, but stopped himself, remembering what his mother said earlier. Instead, he picked up his books. "See you later, Mom," he said as he headed out of the back door.

"Good luck on the team," she responded.

"He'll need it, Mamma. He can't play," laughed Sonny, just loud enough so that Abdul heard him on the porch outside. This was too much for Abdul. He ran back into the house to reach for Sonny. Sonny narrowly escaped by rushing through the front door just in time. Abdul ran after him shouting, "I'm gonna get you, Sonny. Just wait!"

At that moment, Abdul looked down the street just in time to see Tina Brown leaving her home. Tina lived a few doors from Abdul. They had quite a bit in common. Both were 16 years old and both were juniors in high school. They had been friends since kindergarten. Abdul had noticed how sophisticated Tina seemed to look lately. "It's not her glasses," he thought. "I guess it's her natural sophistication. She seems very refined in a sort of African way, I guess."

Tina had just walked out of her front yard and was turning west, down the sidewalk. Abdul ran to catch her. She stopped and turned suddenly and he ran into her, knocking her to the ground. Her books and papers went flying through the air. "Watch where you're going, Abdul", she yelled.

Abdul stood over her with a look of confusion on his face, as his brother Sonny ran past. He seemed lost for words. "Why are you just standing there, Abdul," Sonny called back.

"Oh, I—I'm sorry, Tina," he finally said, reaching down to help her off of the ground. "I was trying to catch up with you," he said apologetically. Tina gave Abdul the evil eye, from behind her bifocals. The glasses made her deep brown eyes appear larger than they were.

"Her eyes look like owl's eyes," thought Abdul, feeling uncomfortable. He lowered his eyes.

Then he moved closer to Tina and tried to brush the dust from the back of her dress. Again, Tina gave him the evil eye again. "Just pick up the books," she finally said. Grinning sheepishly, Abdul slowly picked up her scattered books and papers and handed them to her. They headed for school together, not saying much, as Tina examined her soiled papers. She was still frowning and fussing.

"Abdul, just look at what you did to my homework! Do you know how long it took me to do it? I can't turn it in looking like this!"

"At least you got yours done." Abdul said, not knowing what else to say. "I didn't even do mine."

Tina, a little calmer now, looked at him. "You mean you didn't do your homework," she laughed. "You know if Ms. Hayes flunks you, you won't be able to play basketball anymore."

"What else is new," Abdul faked a laugh. In reality, he felt depressed. "I just can't concentrate anymore," he added. "I haven't been sleeping nights."

Abdul saw a look of compassion in Tina's eyes. Her deep brown eyes looked even larger than before. "What do you think the problem is, Abdul," she asked.

"I don't know. I guess I'll be all right," he said, attempting to smile and look in control. When Tina smiled, Abdul noticed her shiny braces.

As they approached the busy intersection, the traffic sounds gradually filled the morning air, adding vigor to what was once stillness. The warm rays of the sun were now shining through the thick clouds overhead. The sound of a horn caught their attention. It was Slim Perkins. He waved to them as he drove past in his new Nissan.

Abdul noticed Sonia Evans on the passenger side. She was looking out the window. Sonia was considered the most beautiful girl on campus. She was wearing her hair in braids today. Her skin was a deep dark reddish brown. The African bracelet she was wearing looked good against her skin. Her necklace added sparkle to her already sparkling eyes. She was a senior in high school and one of the school's cheerleaders. Abdul felt envious as he watched the Nissan speed away. "Man, I wish I was in Slim's shoes right now," he thought.

Thurgood Marshall High was a very large school. It covered about four square blocks. Most of its buildings were built in the 1930s. The school administrators were proud of the new gym. The gym was large and had all of the latest equipment, including an Olympic-size pool. The gym had cost nearly a quarter of a million dollars.

Abdul could see the dome shape of the gym's ceiling as he headed toward Marshall High School. Abdul walked Tina into the Social Studies building, and over to her locker. He helped her with her books and then started for his Physical Education class. Then he paused for a moment, watching her as she wove through other students who were gathered in the hallway. "She's got a nice shape," he thought. "She just needs to take those glasses off."

Then he turned and headed for the gym.

The gym was well-lit and the floor was smooth and shiny. The wooden bleachers were flat against the walls. From the doorway, Abdul could see several of his teammates shooting baskets with beads of sweat pouring down their dark faces. He watched them for a few moments. Then he walked up to

Al, who was standing on the side line, and asked if the coach was in. Al shrugged and didn't respond, so Abdul yelled to the other players.

"Nope, he's not in," a few of them shouted back at the same time. Abdul picked up a basketball, dribbled a few times, and shot a basket. The ball hit the rim and then bounced off onto the floor.

"You still shooting bricks, Abdul," Dave yelled, laughing. Abdul looked at him with disdain, thinking, "Don't say anything to me, you tall, lanky jerk!" Then he headed for the locker room to change clothes.

As he bent over to tie his tennis shoes, he could hear his teammates stop practicing and start talking excitedly. Immediately, he stepped out to see what was happening. Slim had just walked into the gym, and everyone was gathering around him, shaking his hand, and patting him on his back. "Hey, what's happening, my man," Dave was saying, grinning at Slim.

"Hey fellahs," Slim replied, smiling. He was wearing a dark blue sweat shirt and an expensive looking pair of tennis shoes. He was tall and slender with dark and handsome African features. His dark flashing eyes seemed to drive girls wild. When Abdul spoke, Slim allowed his eyes to roam over Abdul's body from his head to his foot. Then he turned back around and continued talking to the other teammates.

Then Coach Phillips walked in. Phillips was 6'8" and weighed about 250 pounds. He was huge but gentle in his manner. He was patient and humble. When the team made mistakes and got behind, he never seemed to get angry. That is why the guys called him the "Gentle Giant." Others called him "Spock" because he rarely displayed any emotion.

As usual, the coach held basketball practice for one hour during the first period of school and for two hours after school. The coach always started practice with twenty laps around the gym. "All right, let's get busy," the coach yelled, and blew the whistle he was wearing around his neck. When the players heard it, they took off around the perimeter of the court, their feet pounding heavily against the wooden floor. "Let's move it," the coach kept yelling, as the pace picked up.

After about 20 minutes, the coach started the team with wind sprints. After that, he started the shooting, dribbling, blocking out, and passing drills. After these drills, he spent the rest of the time drilling defensive plays. The coach was a strong believer that pressure defense wins games. Scrimmage was always saved for the last part of practice. It was during this time that everyone tried to impress the coach with his individual skills.

He separated the players into two squads for the scrimmage. One squad would be the first string, and the other would be the second string. Abdul was always on the second squad. He didn't like it, but he knew he wasn't good enough to play first string, at least not yet. At the moment, Abdul wasn't quick, agile or very strong. He couldn't shoot or dribble very well and in spite of his height, he wasn't a good rebounder. He wanted to make first string so badly. It didn't matter how hard he needed to practice.

Therefore Abdul knew that the coach didn't consider him a natural basketball player. Abdul realized that he would need to work very hard to change this. So far, it hadn't been easy to do. He had tried lifting weights to gain strength, but he just couldn't get that enthused about it. People were saying that the only reason Coach Phillips kept him on the team was his 6'7" height.

Slim played center on the first string, and seemed to be able to do everything Abdul couldn't do. Slim had experience. It was his senior year, and he had been a starter since the time that he was a freshman. Last season he averaged 32 points per game, and was the conference's leading rebounder.

Slim, like many of the other young players, looked at Michael Jordan as a role model, and patterned most of his moves after Jordan. One of Slim's favorite moves, was a reverse slam dunk. It was a real crowd pleaser. Slim could jump like a seven-footer, even though he was only 6'3" tall.

Soon Abdul and Slim stood in the middle of the court, ready for the tip ball to start the scrimmage. Abdul's eyes were wide with anticipation. He and Slim faced each other with their bodies slightly bent in order to get a better jump. Slim was relaxing and smiling at the crowd. The coach threw the ball into the air.

Slim easily out-jumped Abdul for the tip. Short Red, point guard on the first team, got possession of the ball and dribbled it in for an easy lay-up. Abdul darted, with the other players, back and forth, up and down the court. He could see that the first team was scoring most of the baskets. As he ran, he could hear Coach Phillips shouting directions from the sideline. Every now and then Phillips would stop everyone and correct one of the players.

Abdul was frustrated. He was playing center, but he couldn't score, even though he was traveling constantly. He seemed powerless, as Slim blocked three of his shots and then stole the ball from him at will. Abdul couldn't stop Slim from scoring. He watched Slim drive in on him, pull up for jumpers, and slam him in his face. Anger rose in his throat when Slim yelled at him, "In your face," on the pull-up jumpers. He felt sickened as he heard the whooshing sound of the ball going through the net.

After the scrimmage, the coach went over the plays, diagramming them on the chalkboard in front of the players. Then he dismissed them, and they slowly gathered in the locker room. Exhausted, Abdul started taking off his tennis shoes as he heard the water bursting through the fawcets in the shower room, and the locker room doors opening and slamming. Steam from the open shower stalls covered the room with a hazy fog until the green lockers were barely visible.

Abdul closed his locker and walked toward the showers.

He stepped in and removed the towel he wore around his waist. he had to bend slightly to get under the shower head. When he turned on the fawcet, cold water sprayed his nude body. All around him, he could hear voices, talking and laughing. A good feeling was in the air. It had been a good workout. Abdul looked across the shower to the other shower stall, where Slim was talking to Bryan, another teammate.

"I heard you took Linda to the drive-in last night," Bryan said to Slim.

"No, Linda took me," Slim grinned.

"What about Sonia? You know she's gonna be jealous," Bryan continued, rinsing soap from his body.

"Who cares," Slim said, pushing his chest out with pride. "Nobody has claims on me. I do what I want to, and when I want to do it!" Abdul saw Slim glance in his direction. "Now guys like him," Slim nodded towards Abdul. "They're scared to death of girls." All eyes focused on Abdul. "I heard Tina asked him to take her out, but he was afraid.

Laughter echoed through the showers and through the locker room. Abdul jumped up angrily.

"Stay out of my business, Slim" Abdul shouted at Slim.

"What business," Slim asked, still grinning. "What Tina needs is a real man like me." He pointed toward his chest.

Abdul suddenly lunged towards him. Two of his teammates grabbed him and held him back. As he was struggling to get free, the coach walked in. "OK guys, break it up and get to your classes. I'll see you all after school," he told them.

On the way from the gym, Abdul saw Miss Thompson, the other Physical Education instructor. "Hi, Abdul," she said. As they stood in the doorway of the gym, Abdul had trouble keeping his eyes off of Miss Thompson. Abdul considered her a very unusual woman. She was beautiful, yet she was intelligent. She was also athletic. Abdul could hardly believe that he had found all three of these qualities in one woman. Even though she was a female coach, the male coaches respected her.

She always said things that inspired Abdul to do better. "How are you doing on the basketball team," she asked today. "I'm O.K.," Abdul answered. "I'm still trying to make first string."

Her voice had a serious tone. "If you believe in yourself, Abdul, and if you work hard, you can become anything you want to become. Ever hear of Muhammed Ali? He was about your age when he started working on becoming the greatest fighter who ever lived. He didn't let anything stop him. You shouldn't let anything stop you either."

"I won't," he responded, feeling a little better, but not entirely convinced that he could be like Muhammed Ali.

Marshall High School had a large courtyard located in the center of its campus. Abdul stood in the door leading to the courtyard. His eyes rested on one large oak tree after another. The courtyard reminded him of a small park. The trees were almost bare. Abdul watched as the yellowish brown leaves occasionally fell to the ground. As he walked briskly through the yard, heading for his next class, an autumn breeze was scattering the colorful leaves.

High above, the pale blue sky was becoming cloudy. Through the clouds he could see sunshine still breaking forth. As he continued toward class, he could see students gathering near the exit on the other side of the courtyard. It was recess. He decided to take a walk near the library before actually going to class.

When he reached the library, he saw Slim standing in front of it, on the steps. Three attractive females surrounded Slim. From their expressions alone, one would think that Slim was Prince Charming. Obviously loving the attention, Slim grinned from ear to ear. Abdul felt a familiar tightening in his chest. He was angry again. He walked faster and pretended that he didn't see Slim. He hoped Slim wouldn't see him either. Slim had a habit of always trying to make him look small to others.

As Abdul turned the corner, he breathed a quick sigh of relief. "Why do I allow him to get to me," he thought.

Abdul was late for his English class. He tried to enter, unnoticed, and slip into the back of the room. The teacher, Dr. Hamilton, was talking. When Abdul walked into the room, she narrowed her eyes and gave him the evil eye. Abdul hurried to a seat at the back of the class behind his friend Tina. Tina turned and whispered. "You can't speak, Abdul?"

"Hi, Tina," he said. The teacher cleared her throat and everyone remained silent. She was an elderly woman, her golden colored skin was lined with wrinkles. Her stern face was always without makeup. Nobody knew her exact age, but people joked that she was older than the school. Her students never developed a close relationship with her, for she remained aloof and detached. But in spite of her reserve, she was a very efficient teacher. One of her popular phrases was, "I'm here to develop minds—not friends."

"Okay class, it is now time for your homework assignments. You will recall from yesterday that you were to write essays about your favorite heroes. Today, each person will read his or her essay to the class." A few students sulked. Others sighed. However, she did not hesitate. "You will be graded both on the subject matter and on the presentation itself."

She glanced around the room and then focused on Elizabeth, A tall girl with long blond hair. Elizabeth stood up and walked confidently to the front of the class. Her voice was clear and steady as she read from the paper she held in her hand. Her essay was about Diane Feinstein, the former mayor of San Francisco. Her essay was well organized, and she gave an impressive presentation.

Then Dr. Hamilton glanced around the room again. This time her eyes stopped at Raymond. Raymond was a short, chubby student with a medium brown complexion. His essay was about Supreme Court Justice Thurgood Marshall, the person after whom Marshall High School was named. Raymond explained how important it was for Black people to be judges, lawyers and Supreme Court Justices. He talked about the work that Justice Thurgood Marshall did in the area of Civil Rights. Raymond's presentation was also very well organized and inspirational to the students.

Next, Tina presented her essay about Harriet Tubman. Harriet Tubman was an Abolitionist, who lived during the 19th Century. She was a black woman who helped slaves escape on the famous Underground Railroad. The class listened quietly as Tina explained that the Underground Railraod was a sophisticated network of people called Abolitionists. Abolitionists wanted to make the owning of slaves illegal throughout the United States.

They helped slaves escape from slave states to states where slavery was already illegal. Tubman had risked her life to help slaves escape to Northern free states and to Canada. Several other students read their papers. Then the teacher's eye roamed the room again, and stopped at Abdul.

"I didn't finish my paper," he said, slumping into his seat. The teacher continued calling other students' names and, after the last student read his paper, she dismissed the class. She asked Abdul to remain after class. When the last student closed the door, Dr. Hamilton sat, looking at Abdul with a look of disappointment. Abdul was sitting in the front row, again slumping into the seat.

"Abdul," she said, "Your grades are going from bad to worse." He did not respond. "If you continue in this manner, I'll have no other choice but to flunk you."

Abdul shifted in his seat, feeling uncomfortable. His hands fumbled with the buttons on his sweater, as he searched for something to say. He knew he had no excuse. He knew that his mind wasn't on anything but basketball. "Do you have anything to say, Abdul," Dr. Hamilton asked.

"No Ma'am," he replied.

"Well, I guess I'll have a conference with your parents, then."

Abdul sat up suddenly. "My mother can't come!" he snapped.

"Why not," she asked.

Abdul answered, taking a deep breath, and trying to keep his voice low. "She works all day."

"What about your father?" she asked.

"My father died in a car accident when I was ten years old." His voice was so low that Dr. Hamilton could barely hear him.

Abdul stared at the floor, but felt her eyes continuing to study him, but this time, with compassion.

"Sorry to hear that," she replied sympathetically. "But I must speak with your mother." She signed a form letter, placed it in an envelope, and asked Abdul to give it to his mother.

On the way to his next class, Abdul wondered what to do about his grades. He was behind in three classes: English, Algebra, and Social Studies. "It isn't that I can't do the work," he thought. "My mind just isn't on studying."

He knew he must get at least an average grade in all of his classes. In any event, he didn't like the idea of his mother coming down to the school. "What'll it look like for my mother to come down here to the school," he asked himself, as he walked into his Algebra class.

The day seemed to drag as he went from one class to another, waiting for his last class to end, so that he could go to basketball practice. As he was leaving his last class, he saw Tina in the hallway getting her books from her locker.

"Hi, Tina," he said, walking toward her.

"Hi, Abdul," she spoke, while struggling with her stack of books. Abdul reached over and helped her remove the books from her locker.

"I would help you carry them home, but I have to go to practice," he said.

"That's okay," she said softly, smiling and looking at him

with her dark brown eyes. "Did you decide what to do about your grades?"

"Not yet," he answered. Suddenly he got an idea. "Do you think you can help me, Tina," he asked.

"Of course," she answered. "I'll ask my mother if I can come over and help you tonight."

"What would I do without you, Tina! You are the sweetest girl on earth," Abdul sang as he put on his jacket.

"Umm-huh, you always say that when you want something," Tina laughed.

Later, as Abdul was entering the gym, he saw Coach Phillips talking to Miss Thomas, the other Physical Education Instructor. She reminded him of pictures of "Flo Jo" the Olympic champion. "That's a real woman," he thought. They both looked up as Abdul approached, and the coach said, "Abdul, I need to see you in my office."

Abdul spoke to Miss Thompson and headed toward the Coach's office, which was located inside the gym next to the locker room. The door was open so he entered and sat down on a sofa across from a big mahogany desk. His eyes surveyed the trophy-filled room. He focused on a large trophy with a two-foot silver cup. It was sitting in a glass case which covered the full length of the back wall,

Letters engraved in gold on it read: STATE CHAMPIONSHIP 1989.

His mind wandered to Coach Phillips. What was taking him so long? Nervously, he ran his hands over the smooth surface of the leather sofa.

Suddenly Coach Phillips entered the room. His voice cut into the silence. "We've got to do something about your grades, Abdul." Abdul jumped as though he'd been caught in the act of stealing. The coach looked at him and squinted his eyes.

"Your counselor called me today and said you're behind in most of your classes. He said that if you don't improve, the school will have to remove you from the team. I told him I'd have a talk with you before practice."

Abdul sat in silence with his head slumped over. "What's the problem, Son," Coach Phillips asked. "You were doing real well until recently." Abdul looked away from Coach Phillips out the window, but he could feel the coach's black eyes continuing to probe him.

"I'm all right Coach." He paused. "I just haven't been able to concentrate."

"Any problems at home," the coach asked.

"Nope," Abdul answered.

"How is your mother," the coach continued.

"She's fine," Abdul answered, managing a smile.

"Well, you just have to study harder, Abdul, and if I can help, you know I'm always available, the coach added.

"Thanks, Coach, but Tina is suppose to come over and help me tonight," Abdul said. The coach patted him on the shoulders and they left the office, heading for practice. Practice went as usual, with the first string dominating and Slim highlighting the game. When Slim pulled up for a jump-shot, his voice echoed through the gym—"In your face, sucker!"

Chapter Two

When Abdul arrived home from practice, he made a sandwich and sat down to study Algebra. It was 5:30 p.m. and his mother hadn't come home from work. Sonny was watching television in the front room. His mother had decorated the living room in beige and white.

A long couch, upholstered in an African print with a matching love seat was on one side of the room. In front of the couch was a large rectangular black coffee table with a thick glass top. Several magazines were stacked neatly on top of it. A large tree plant was in a far corner, and adjacent to the couch was a large floor model television. Next to it was a new stereo- system.

Abdul sat down at the kitchen table and worked on a few Algebra problems, but closed the book in frustration. Then he finished his sandwich and went to watch television with Sonny. "What you watching, little Bro?"

"Cartoons" Sonny replied, his eyes focused on the television screen.

"All you ever watch is cartoons," Abdul said. "Let's watch the sports channel."

"No, cartoons," Sonny said, with his eyes still glued to the television screen. Abdul got up and turned the channel anyway. Then Sonny charged into him like a mad bull. His arms started swinging furiously.

Abdul grabbed him and wrestled him to the floor.

"Cool it Sonny," Abdul, almost out of breath.

"You started it!" Sonny said angrily. "I was watching TV first!"

"Okay—okay, you can watch your dumb cartoons." Abdul said, releasing Sonny and storming upstairs. Sonny went back to watch cartoons, just as his mother walked in the front door.

"Hi Mom," Sonny spoke, with his eyes still staring at the screen.

"Hi, Baby," she said. Sonny noticed that she looked tired after working eight hours. She seemed happy to be home.

"Where's your brother," she asked.

"He's upstairs, " Sonny answered.

Sonny and Abdul were very proud of their mother. They knew it wasn't easy for her to take care of two boys without a husband. She did very well with such a small income. She worked as a secretary for one of the city's prominent Black civil rights attorneys, James Streeter.

He had reached national acclaim after winning a job discrimination case against the Sun Corporation, a company that was found guilty of deliberately passing over qualified blacks to promote less qualified whites. His mother had been working for Attorney Streeter for almost ten years. She started as a legal aid. Then, after taking some night classes in Business Administration, she got a promotion to the position of executive secretary. Then the family moved from the projects to a new home.

Abdul, Sonny, and his mother were relieved to move out of the projects, away from drugs, gangs, and violence. They lived in the Oak Park area of Sacramento, where many Black families owned homes and worked very hard to build a healthy neighborhood. So far, they were succeeding.

When Abdul heard his mother come in from work, he came down stairs. He glanced at her to detect her mood. She was sitting down reading the day's mail when he walked into the living room. The light from the table lamp was casting soft shadows across her face. Other than being a little tired, she seemed in a good mood. "Hi, Mom. How'd it go at work today?"

"Oh, it went okay, Son," she answered. "How was school?"

"Okay, " he said quickly.

He glanced over at Sonny who was still immersed in the television. He didn't want Sonny to know about the note from Dr. Hamilton, so he decided to give it to his mother later, after Sonny was out of sight.

The telephone rang and Abdul started toward the kitchen

to answer it, but Sonny ran past him and picked it up. "Johnson residence, Sonny speaking," he answered, holding the phone with both hands. "Hi Tina!"

"I'm fine," he continued. "Yeah, he's here. Just a moment." He handed Abdul the telephone. Abdul was standing next to him frowning. He snatched the telephone from Sonny and raised his hand to feign a blow. "Get out of here" he shouted. Sonny ducked out of the way. He poked out his tongue and ran to the front room."

Abdul cleared his throat as if preparing for a long speech. "Billy Dee Williams speaking", he finally said. "What can I do for you?"

"Abdul, you're crazy. Don't you ever get serious," Abdul heard Tina say on the other end."

"Once in a while," he teased. "What did your mother say?"

"She said I can come over. But I can only stay a couple of hours," she added.

"Well," Abdul joked, "that's plenty of time for us to make love."

"Abdul, I'm coming over to help you with your lessons and that's all," Tina laughed. "If you start that mess like you did last time, I will leave."

Abdul thought about the last time Tina had come over to help him with his school work. His mother and Sonny had to leave on an unexpected errand and left Abdul and Tina alone. After they finished the school work, they sat on the couch talking and listening to music. Then they started kissing and necking. Abdul got excited and tried to go farther than Tina would allow.

Tina pushed him away, and jumped up, yelling, "Stop! I told you I didn't want to go all of the way!" She smoothed her skirt down, brushed her hair, and left, while Abdul pleaded with her to stay.

"I promise to be a perfect gentleman this time," Abdul said, knowing that Tina remembered the earlier incident.

"You better, Abdul," Tina said, with a smile.

"Hey, Tina," Abdul said just before hanging up the telephone. "Don't forget to bring your new Public Enemy album. I want to practice a little for the dance.

"Okay," she agreed. "See you later."

Abdul hung the telephone up and went back into the front room. Sonny had gone upstairs, leaving his mother watching the evening news.

"Mom, I got something to give you." Abdul said, handing her the note. He sat down on the couch beside her and crossed his long legs. He wondered what she was thinking as she read the note in silence, but her soft face was without expression. After what seemed like an eternity, she put the note down on the table and leaned back on the couch. Her brown eyes looked earnestly at Abdul. He fidgeted and scratched his head.

"Abdul, why didn't you tell me you were behind in your classes," she asked.

"I'm only a little behind," he mumbled.

"A little bit," she asked, raising her voice.

Abdul was silent.

"I guess I'll have to take off from work to see about this," she finally said. Abdul looked at her numbly, feeling self-pity and at a loss for words.

The door bell rang and Abdul went to answer it. "Who is it," he asked, speaking through the small hole in the door.

"It's me, Abdul," said a high pitched voice. Abdul recognized it. It was Bo Edwards. Bo was his best friend. They grew up together. Bo also played basketball. Like Abdul, he was on the second string.

Bo was about 5'9". He had a muscular build, and his legs were slightly bowed. He wore his hair short and it was neatly parted on both sides. Even rows of silky waves of hair covered his head. He had a broad nose and thick lips, and his even white teeth were always visible. Unlike Abdul, who usually wore tennis shoes and jeans, Bo always wore slacks and designer shoes. Bo and Abdul were almost complete opposites in appearance and personality.

Bo was outgoing and flamboyant. However, Abdul was quiet and withdrawn. Abdul's mother said that the reason they probably got along so well was that "opposites attract".

Abdul opened the door and Bo walked in, swaggering. "Hey, what's happening, my man," Bo said with a ritual handshake.

"Nothing much," Abdul answered. "Come on in." Bo was wearing grey slacks and a black cashmere sweater. His shoes were so shiny that they looked like patent leather. He was holding a small brush that he used to keep his hair wavy. Bo walked into the front room where Abdul's mother was still watching television.

"Hi, Ms. Johnson." he spoke.

"Hi, Bo. How are you doing," she said, smiling.

"I'm fine," he answered.

"How're your mother and father," she asked.

"Oh, fine, he answered.

Bo lived in an exclusive area of Sacramento called Green Haven. Bo's father was a successful real estate investor who owned numerous homes throughout the city. His father always wore three-piece suits and every year he bought a new Mercedes. Their Green Haven home was a large split-level house, with a swimming pool in the backyard. Every room looked like something a person would find in a magazine.

"Why weren't you at practice today?" Abdul asked as Bo sat down on the love seat, brushing his hair.

"I had to go to the dentist to have my grill checked," Bo showed his teeth. "What did you guys do today?" Bo asked.

"Same as always. We went through some drills and some plays. Then we had a scrimmage." Abdul reported. "You know we got a game Saturday night."

"Yeah, but there won't be much action for us to see," Bo

replied, still stroking his hair with the brush.

"You said that right! We'll be warming the bench as usual," Abdul responded.

"Don't worry about it." his mother interrupted. "You both still have another year to play."

"Yeah", Bo said. "But that's a long time to be warming the bench. Anyway I got to go," he said, standing and moving toward the door. Abdul walked him to the door and watched Bo as he strutted toward his father's maroon Mercedes, parked at the curb.

While Bo was leaving, another car drove up and Tina got out from the passenger's side. Tina's mother was behind the wheel. Abdul waved at Tina's mother. Then her mother sped away in her red Thunderbird with her tires squealing. Abdul could see Tina's mother's reddish wig as the light from the moon fell onto the front seat of the car. The wig hung down to her shoulders.

Abdul couldn't understand why she wore a wig. her real hair was already long enough. His mind returned to Tina as she walked up onto the porch, carrying several books and record albums.

"Hi, Abdul. Was that Bo I saw leaving," Tina asked.

"Yeah," Abdul said.

"I didn't see him at school today," she said.

"He had to go to the dentist," Abdul replied, holding the front door open for her. They went inside and sat down in the front room. Then Tina greeted Abdul's mother, who was in the kitchen preparing dinner.

"Hello, Tina," she said, seeming happy to see her. "That's a pretty blouse you are wearing."

"Thank you, Ms. Johnson." Tina replied. Abdul's mother had told him that she liked Tina because Tina was well-mannered, and because she didn't drink, smoke, or "do drugs". His mother had seen Tina at church on Sundays. She liked the way Tina dressed. She had encouraged Abdul to date Tina, but Abdul said she wasn't his type.

Tina and her mother lived alone. Her father had left them when she was a baby. She didn't remember anything about him, but she heard rumors that he was once a wealthy pimp. Tina's mother ran a successful soul food restaurant in Oak Park. The restaurant was a first-class establishment, serving clientele throughout the city and suburbs. People traveled several miles to eat her gumbo and southern barbecue. Tina's mother had a warm personality which caused people to be attracted to her. Tina worked in her mother's restaurant on weekends, helping her mother to cook and serve customers. Tina and her mother looked alike. Sometimes people thought they were sisters. The only difference between them was that Tina's mother wore a wig.

Tina helped him work one Algebra problem after another. Abdul didn't have any problems understanding the work. His problem was retaining what he'd learned. He kept forgetting the rules regarding positive and negative signs. But after Tina went over it with him several times. Then he began to re-member. After they completed the Algebra chapter, Tina helped Abdul with his essay on his favorite hero for his En-glish class. At first Abdul couldn't name any heroes other than basketball players. He told Tina that he wanted to write a paper on "Doctor J". However, Tina convinced him to select someone who contributed something more significant to Black American history than athletes had contributed. Then Tina suggested Toussaint L'Ouverture, who waged the war that eventually freed Haiti from slavery. When Abdul learned about L'Ouverture, he was highly impressed, and decided to write about him.

When they finished studying, Abdul put on a record so Tina could show him some new dance steps. Tina may have been plain in her appearance, but there was nothing plain about the way she danced. Her body moved in ways which seemed almost humanly impossible. She moved with the grace and

elegance of a professional dancer, but she almost had the same skill as an African dancer.

Abdul attempted to dance with her but was clumsy and out of step. His mother and Sonny came downstairs when they heard the music and joined the fun. Sonny started dancing like M. C. Hammer. He knew all the latest steps and moves.

When Sonny danced with Tina, she mimicked each one of his moves with perfect timing, as though they had been practicing for years. Abdul's mother joined in and tried to show them the Lindy-Hop, a dance that was popular when she was a teenager. They were all dancing, laughing, and having a good time, when they heard a car horn blowing outside. Tina looked at her watch.

"That must be my mother." she said, gathering her books and albums. Abdul walked her to the car.

Later that night when Abdul went to bed, he had a dream that he had had before. In the dream, his team was playing a championship game in front of a sellout crowd. They were behind the other team score by one point. Ten seconds remained in the game. Slim had fouled out. The coach didn't have any choice but to put Abdul in the game. The capacity crowd was yelling, "Abdul! Abdul!" The coach had called a time-out to prepare a strategy, which involved a set play to Abdul.

"I'm putting you in the game, Abdul," Coach Phillips said, in the dream. "The entire championship depends on you." Abdul nodded his head. He looked around nervously feeling his throat turn dry. In the dream, he found himself wishing he was somewhere else—anywhere but at the game.

The crowd continued to cheer and chant his name. The noise filled the entire gym. The electricity drove up the player's adrenaline. Then the buzzer sounded, ending the time-out. Abdul rushed to the floor with the other players. He felt the championship weighing heavily on his shoulder. The coach designed the plays so that Abdul could come off of a felt the championship weighing heavily on his shoulder. The coach designed the plays so that Abdul could come off of a pick from the baseline to the top of the key, with an option to take a jumper or drive to the basket.

When the game resumed, everything went as planned. Abdul came off a pick, then maneuvered to the top of the key, where he received the ball. But when he turned to face the basket, one of his opponents denied him the "jumper". However, to his surprise, the lane was wide open! In his dream, it was so wide that, not only could he win the game, he could win it in style!

His heart pumped with excitement as he prepared himself for the drive. Beads of sweat rolled down his face, and his muscles tightened. He put the ball down on the floor and began dribbling towards the basket. The lane was still wide open as he became airborne at the top of the key. He could hear the shouts of his teammates over the loud roar of the crowd, as he glided through the air.

"Slam it, Abdul! Slam it," the crowd shouted. He held the ball, palmed in one hand, high over his head, and floated in the air for a time that, in his dream, seemed to last forever. A big smile slowly appeared on his face as he neared the basket, preparing for the slam. Just as he was about to dunk the ball, to his horror, a looming figure appeared suddenly from nowhere. It was a grinning apparition of Slim. Laughing loudly, he rejected the ball, sending it viciously back into Abdul's face.

Abdul awoke suddenly from his dream, with sweat running down his forehead. He rested on his back, thinking about his dream. In a way, he wished that he wouldn't have these types of dreams anymore. It seemed that he had this disturbing dream almost every night. Finally, after much tossing and turning, he went back to sleep.

Chapter Three

The next morning Abdul woke up early, eager to get to school. He was anxious to present his essay on Toussaint L'Ouverture. On the way to school, Tina told Abdul more about Toussaint and his role in the Haitian revolution. When they reached school, he thanked her again and watched as she disappeared through the crowd across the campus.

As he turned to go, he saw Slim talking to Sonia and another girl he'd never seen. She was quite sensuous, Abdul noticed. She had on a revealing halter and a pair of Jordache jeans that hugged her round bottom.

She had large, soft-looking lips, which she covered with a sensuous dark lipstick. "Too much," Abdul thought, as he studied her more closely.

"Hey Abdul," Slim yelled. "I want you to meet someone."

Abdul looked uncomfortable as he walked slowly toward them. He spoke to Sonia, then to a new girl who was staring at him with keen interest. When girls looked at him like that, he always felt uneasy. He didn't know if it was because they liked him or because they thought he looked odd.

"Abdul, this is my cousin Diane." Sonia said, "She's from Los Angeles."

"Hi, Abdul." Diane smiled mischievously, her hazel eyes gazing up at Abdul.

"Hello, Diane," Abdul said, shifting nervously and giving her a shy smile.

"Are you on the basketball team," she asked.

"Yeah, I'm on the team," he grinned.

"I bet you're good," she said, smiling.

He didn't know if she was serious or joking. "I play all right," he said, trying to determine her intentions. She moved closer. He smelled her perfume.

"Abdul, I think you're so tall and handsome," she said sweetly. Abdul blushed, not knowing how to respond. He shyly lowered his eyes. Slim turned away and put his hand over his mouth to restrain a laugh. Sonia hit him playfully.

"Are you going to the dance after the game Saturday?" Diane asked Abdul.

"I was planning to go," Abdul answered.

"Will you take me," she asked boldly.

"He looked at her, surprised. Abdul couldn't believe his ears. "She wants me to take her to the dance," he thought. His voice broke and he swallowed.

"You want me to take you to the dance," he said out loud.

"Yes. Will you," she repeated.

"I guess so," he answered.

"What do you mean you guess so," Slim interrupted. "Are you taking her or not?"

"Sure, sure. I'm taking her," Abdul snapped glaring at Slim.

"Well, then, I'll see you Saturday night, my-man," Slim said, strolling away. The threesome left, leaving Abdul deep in thought. He wondered what Tina would think when she found out that he was taking Diane to the dance. Tina had asked him numerous times to go to the dance with him. However, he'd always found some excuse not to take her. He recognized that she was a good dancer, and was probably the best at school, but she didn't "look" like girls you take to a dance.

She had braces and she wore her dresses below her knees. As he started for home, he also remembered the promise he had made to Bo about going to the dance with him. Bo would understand. At least he hoped Bo would.

That evening they had a light practice. The coach spent most of the time on defensive drills. Afterwards, Abdul showered quickly and then waited outside for Bo, to tell him about his date with Diane. Bo was walking from the gym, brushing his hair, when Abdul called him.

"What's up Abdul," Bo asked.

"I'm not going to the dance with you on Saturday night," Abdul said.

"What? You on punishment or something," Bo asked, as they walked from the gym.

"No, that's not it," Abdul replied.

"Well, what's wrong," Bo kept on pushing.

Abdul hesitated before speaking, "I'm taking Diane to the dance."

"Diane," Bo asked with surprise. "Who's Diane?"

Abdul's face lit up. "Diane's the new girl from Los Angeles."

You mean Sonia's cousin," Bo asked. You got to be kidding, man!"

"No, she asked me to take her," Abdul said, boasting.

Bo stopped walking and looked Abdul straight in his eyes. "She asked you?"

"Yep," Abdul grinned.

"You don't even know her," Bo said, raising his voice.

"So," Abdul replied.

"I think you're making a big mistake, Man. She looks a little too experienced, if you know what I mean," Bo added, after a moment's silence.

"I hope you're not angry because I changed my mind," Abdul said.

"No, it's cool, but you'll be sorry, my-man," Bo laughed.

Later, when Abdul walked into his English class he took a seat in the front row. Dr. Hamilton was sitting behind her desk. She looked up over her rimmed glasses at Abdul. He had never sat in the front row during the entire semester.

Dr. Hamilton seemed to doubt his sincerity. Abdul looked around the room for Tina. She was sitting near the back, staring at him through her thick glasses. She smiled at him warmly. He wondered if she knew about his date with Diane, but quickly dismissed the thought when the teacher started talking.

"Today we will allow time for those students who didn't present their essays earlier. Do I have any volunteers?" Abdul quickly raised his hand, sitting on the edge of his seat. "I'm ready to read my paper," he said, excitedly.

She studied him a few seconds, then signaled him forward. Abdul had an air of confidence as he walked up to face the class. The entire class seemed to expect that something good was about to happen. Abdul stood erect, with his eyes gleaming. He saw Tina giving him an encouraging smile from the back of the room. Abdul cleared his throat and began to read. "The title of my paper is Toussaint L'Ouverture: the Man who Liberated Haiti."

Everyone, including the teacher, looked at him with questions in their eyes, wondering who Toussaint L'Ouverture was. Abdul explained that L'Ouverture fought against what were once the main superpowers of the world, when they attempted to dominate Haiti. He explained that, during that time, these superpowers wanted to continue holding the Black people of Haiti as slaves. L'Ouverture organized an army of ex-slaves to defeat Emperor Napoleon's well equipped army.

As a result of this defeat, France, eventually had to sell its Louisiana Territories to the United States. The class was surprised to hear that a Black man, particularly an ex-slave, could accomplish all of that. Abdul explained that, as a result of L'Ouverture, Haiti eventually became the first independent Black nation in the Western Hemisphere.

When Abdul returned to his seat, the teacher nodded with approval.

Later, in the cafeteria, Abdul and Tina talked about the presentation while they ate hamburgers and french fries. The lunchroom was becoming crowded and sounds of laughter and small talk, mixed with the clattering of lunch trays, filled the room with interesting noises and smells. Abdul glanced up as Slim, Sonia, and Diana walked into the cafeteria. They were receiving the type of attention that movie stars usually get.

"Who's the new girl," Tina asked, whispering and watching Abdul's face.

"I think her name is Diane." Abdul answered, as if not interested. The threesome picked up their trays and sat down at a table adjacent to Tina and Abdul. Diane looked at Abdul with her large brown eyes. Then she waved and smiled. Abdul returned a half smile and then fidgeted with his hamburger, trying to avoid Tina's suspicious eyes.

Abdul could see a small group of students, gathering at Slim's table, shaking his hand, and wishing him luck for Saturday night's game. Slim grinned from ear to ear, and boasted loudly so that people as far away as Abdul could hear.

After school the team met inside the gym to receive their game plan for Saturday night. Coach Phillips never practiced before a game. He used this time to allow his players to rest and to prepare them mentally and emotionally for the game. The players disliked these sessions, considering them dull and unnecessary. However, Phillips placed great emphasis on the sessions, pointing out that basketball is primarily mental and emotional.

"If you're not mentally or emotionally in the game," he said, "your chances of winning are slight." No one argued with the coach because his consistently winning record supported his philosophy. In his seven years with the team, he coached them through five Regional Championships and one State Championship. The local athletic board named him "Coach of the Year" twice.

A Big Ten college had offered him an assistant coaching position, but he remained at Marshall High school. His friends and colleagues were critical of his decision. They said he missed an opportunity of a life time. They told him this offer was an open door to a head coaching position and possibly to a professional career. However, he'd responded in his nonchalant way, "I like working with these kids, best."

Standing before the chalkboard, the coach went over the game plan in his meticulous manner, stopping now and then to answer the players' questions. The coach considered the team they were to play, an average team. However he emphasized that they should never take an opponent lightly.

For two hours, he reviewed basic rules of discipline, desire and hustle, until he felt that he had imbedded in them a winning attitude. Then he dismissed them with his usual cliche, "A winning team has a winning attitude."

While Abdul and Bo were leaving the gym, Abdul playfully mimicked the coach. "All right, Bo, I want a lot of hustle from you on the bench tomorrow night. It takes a lot of desire to sit there all night," Abdul laughed. "All you need is winning attitude." They both laughed and headed for home.

When Abdul arrived at home, Sonny, had his eyes glued to the television set, as usual. Abdul sat down at the kitchen table and thought about his date with Diane. "Boy, she is so fine," he thought. "Bo didn't know what he was talking about when he said I'd be sorry. He was probably jealous because he couldn't take her. I can hang with him any day."

"But what about Tina," he continued thinking. "She'll be angry because I didn't ask her. Oh, Well, Tina's just a friend and I don't have any commitments to her."

Finally, he decided to call and tell her about his date with Diane. He felt that she would discover it anyway. He glanced at the clock above the stove. It was 4:55 p.m. He still had time to reach Tina before she left for work. He picked up the telephone and dialed her number.

"Yo, what's happening," he asked.

"Not much. I'm just getting ready for work," she replied.

Abdul hesitated, thinking about how he would tell her. "Are you going to the dance tomorrow?" Tina asked.

He thought about lying to her but changed his mind, knowing she would find out anyway. "Yes," he said in a low voice. "Diane asked me to take her."

"Diane," Tina said, "You mean the girl we saw in the cafeteria? Sonia's cousin?"

"Yeah, her." Abdul said, as though Diane was unimportant.

"Well, are you going to take her," she asked.

"I think so," he said.

There was a long silence. Finally Tina said, "That sure is cold, Abdul." She seemed angry, hanging up with out saying goodbye, and leaving Abdul holding the telephone in his hand. He looked at the telephone for a long time before putting it down. He wondered if he should call her and apologize. "No," he told himself. "She will get over it."

Later that evening Tina didn't come to help Abdul with his lessons. Abdul decided to call and ask her what happened. "She's in her room and doesn't want to be disturbed," her mother said over the telephone.

The next morning was Saturday, and Abdul woke up earlier than usual, so that he could go over to Tina's house. When he arrived, Tina's mother was just driving into the driveway.

"Is Tina home," he asked.

"You just missed her Abdul," her mother said. "She's spending the night with her cousin. I just dropped her off."

Abdul knew that Tina was trying to avoid him, but he didn't say anything about it to her mother. Tina's mother got out of the car and watched him walk away. Abdul suspected that Tina's mother knew that he and Tina had probably had a fight.

Abdul spent the rest of the day around the house, listening to tapes and thinking about his date with Diane. He didn't care much about the game, because he knew he wouldn't get to play much—if at all. He thought about calling Diane to cancel the date but dismissed the idea. He knew that Slim would tell everyone on campus that he was afraid.

Finally, he went to his closet to determine what he would wear. He tried on a suit and stood in front of the mirror. Then he took it off and tried on another one. Finally, he decided to wear slacks and a leather jacket. He spent a few minutes shining his shoes, and then went to bed.

The basketball game was to begin at 7:00 p.m. at Burbank High School, located on the south side of Sacramento. Marshall High School's players drove up to Burbank in a mini school bus driven by Coach Phillips. Near the front, four cheerleaders dressed in shorts and sweaters, with pom-poms in their laps, sat near Slim, competing for his attention. Miss Thompson, who supervised the cheerleaders, sat directly behind the coach. The cheerleaders and Ms. Thompson accompanied the team on most of their trips.

When the players entered the locker room, fans began to fill the court. "Hey Slim, what you gonna do tonight," one fan yelled. Then a group of females saw Slim, and screamed, "Slim, Baby!"

From the door leading to the court, Abdul could see the opposing team starting their lay-ups to warm themselves for the game. Their white uniforms had cougars on them. Marshall wore blue and gold with a bear as an emblem.

Later, during Marshall's warm up, Slim did several slam dunks to please the crowd. The crowd cheered and yelled.

In the first half, Burbank remained relatively close, playing good defense and moving the ball well on offense. The first half ended with Marshall High leading 45 to 40. During the second half, Marshall's superior talent began to show. Soon they dominated the game. The final score was 99 to 78, Slim scored 32 points, 17 rebounds and 5 blocked shots. Bo and Abdul played in the last 2 minutes of the game. They both turned the ball over several times. Abdul got a three second call and missed an easy lay-up. Nevertheless, both Bo and Abdul felt happy to get some playing time.

After the game, loud chatter filled the locker room as the players bragged about their victory and about the upcoming dance at the Community Center. "You still taking Diane to the dance," Slim asked Abdul.

"Yeah," Abdul responded, wishing Slim would stay out of his business.

"Well, I'll see you there," Slim said, grinning.

It was early Saturday night and the air was damp and cold.

A full moon peeped through the dark clouds, as if looking down at Abdul. Abdul drove his mother's Cutlass out of the driveway and headed toward Diane's house. He looked at himself in the rear view mirror, as he primped and patted his hair to make sure he looked all right. He wore his hair in a short Afro, parted on the side.

He turned on the car radio and pushed the buttons to find a "Soul" station. Suddenly, an old Temptation's song blared from the radio, "Get ready. Here I come . . ." Abdul smiled, popped his fingers, and began singing along with the music.

He parked in front of a white stucco house with a wooden shingled roof. The grass was freshly cut, enclosed in a five feet steel-linked fence. A "Beware of the Dog" sign was on the gate. Abdul studied the sign, and then the yard. He wondered if he should get out of the car. Thinking that it would be better to be safe than sorry, Abdul blew the horn.

Someone peaked out of the bedroom window. The lights flicked off. Then Diane appeared at the front door. When she stepped off the porch, a large Doberman, with a smooth black coat, came out of the darkness. The dog followed her, and then stood like a statue while she opened and closed the gate.

Diane had on a red sheer dress with a slit up the side. When she opened the car door and sat down, the split revealed her shapely brown legs. The air was sweet with the lingering scent of her perfume as she reached to kiss Abdul softly on his lips. He complimented her on how attractive she looked, then drove toward the dance.

On the way, Diane took out a reefer, lit it and took a long drag. Abdul thought it was a cigarette until he smelled the pungent scent of marijuana. When she passed it to him he didn't know whether to accept it or to refuse. He didn't want to appear a "square", so he took a few puffs. Then he coughed and passed it back to her. She smiled at him mischievously.

"You all right Abdul," she said.

"Yea-yeah, sure—I'm okay," he lied. The smoke was causing

him to cough, and it was making him feel extremely light headed. By the time they reached the dance, they'd smoke two reefers.

People crowded the dance floor. There was hardly standing room. People were bumping, pushing, and shoving to get to the dance floor. Cigarette smells, perfume and sweating bodies filled the air and gave the place a rather rank odor. Trip- lights blinked off and on, causing the dancer's movements to appear stocchatic and rhythmical.

Abdul glanced around at the tables that were clustered together on one side of the dance floor. He noticed a vacant table in a far corner. He held Diane's hand as they moved through the crowd, to the table. When they reached the table and sat down, Diane lit another reefer and passed it to Abdul. He was still feeling high from the second one, but he took the third one anyway. He took a couple of long drags, suppressed the urge to cough and passed it back to Diane. When Diane finished smoking the reefer, her brown eyes were misty.

"How you doing, baby," she slurred.

"I'm feeling real good, real good," he slurred back.

"Me too," she said, repeating herself several times. "Let's dance."

The D.J. had just put on a slow record and couples gradually drifted onto the floor. Abdul embraced Diane, and began moving to the music's slow beat. He put his hand around her small waist and held her close. He was much taller than she was, so he had to bend over slightly. Except for occasionally stepping or her toes, he danced very well. The marijuana had given him a false sense of confidence.

Back at the table, Diane and Abdul laughed continuously, inserting jokes here and there, watching other couples dance.

"Where in Los Angeles are you from," Abdul asked. He was leaning back in his chair, watching Diane with fascination.

"Compton," she said.

"Isn't that where all the gangs are," he asked.

"Gangs are everywhere, baby," she answered. She took a filter-tipped cigarette from her purse and lit it. Her brown eyes suddenly turned cold and hard.

"My girlfriend was killed by the Bloods," she added.

Abdul's eyes registered surprise. "How did it happen? Was she in a gang," he asked.

"No, Sweety," she responded, her voice sounding a little irritated. "She was an innocent bystander." She took a long smoke from her cigarette, seemingly in deep thought. Finally she spoke, "It happened after school one day. My two girl friends, Sheila and Sandra, were walking home. About a block away from school, this car full of Bloods pulled up and started shooting." She paused.

"They were shooting at some boys walking in back of us. The bullet hit my friend Sheila in the chest." Again she paused, with a sad look on her face. "She died on the way to the hospital."

There was an awkward silence and Abdul felt an uncontrollable emotion swelling within. "Did they catch the guys who did it," he asked.

"No—they never do," she said. "When they do, they don't do much time," she said, bitterly.

"What position do you play on the team," she asked, changing the subject.

"I'm the center.—the back-up center behind Slim," Abdul answered with embarrassment.

Diane looked away. "Speaking of Slim, here he comes now." Abdul looked around just as Slim approached the table where they were sitting."

"How are you two love birds doing," Slim asked. He winked at Diane and flashed a grin. Abdul felt his insides tighten, and he looked at Slim with contempt. Slim had on a pair of pleated slacks and a tweed sports jacket."

"We're doing just fine," Abdul answered. He looked around

the room. "Where is Sonia?""

"I took her home. We got into a hassle," Slim said.

Abdul started to ask what the hassle about, but dismissed the idea, considering it none of his business.

"Can I dance with your lady?" Slim asked.

Abdul nodded toward Diane. "You have to ask Diane. I don't have any ties on her."

"May I?" Slim asked Diane. She was sitting with her hands cupped on the table, smiling warmly at Slim.

"Yes, I don't mind," she said sweetly.

Abdul's face clouded with anger, as he watched them dance gracefully on the floor to a slow record, Diane's head rested on Slim's chest.

"Hey, man, everything all right?" Bo's voice came suddenly from nowhere.

"Oh—hi Bo!" Abdul responded, looking across at Bo, who'd taken Diane's seat.

"You okay?" Bo repeated.

"Yeah, Bo, everything's cool," Abdul responded. "How long you been at the dance?"

"I've been here about an hour." Bo replied, staring into Abdul's eyes.

"You been smoking that stuff," Bo asked. "Your eyes look like cat eyes."

Abdul shifted in his seat and tried to avoid Bo's stare. "I only smoked a little. Just trying it out."

Bo shook his head from side to side. "Abdul, that stuff will mess you up".

"No, I can handle it," Abdul said.

Bo was about to respond when he noticed Slim and Diane returning from the dance floor. Bo didn't care much for Slim's company either, so he told Abdul goodbye and left. Slim escorted Diane to the table and disappeared among the crowd.

When Diane sat down, she pulled out a half-pint of Scotch from her purse. Abdul wondered what else she had in her little purse, as she sat the purse on the seat beside her. She sent Abdul to get cups at the refreshment table. Then she headed toward the rest room. When she returned they both began sipping the Scotch. Abdul grimaced when he took a sip, the drink burning his throat. "Aren't you going to mix it," he asked, putting the cup down, and spilling some of the liquid on the table.

"Mix it," she asked, teasingly. "You don't ruin good scotch, sweetheart."

As the evening slowly passed, Abdul's head began to buzz. His vision became cloudy and he walked with a slight stagger. He leaned back in his seat and watched Diane through half-closed eyes. Diane was looking around impatiently. "Let's do some socializing, Baby," she finally said.

"What do you think we're doing," Abdul responded with a slur.

"I mean—let's do our own thing for a while," she said.

Abdul looked at her with a blank expression. She gave him a quick kiss and vanished into the crowd. Abdul sat slumped in his seat, his head bobbing from side to side, looking around the smoke-filled room. He tried to find Bo in the crowd, but all he could see was a blurry mass of figures, moving in time with the music.

He stood up and staggered away from the table. As he moved, he caught a glimpse of some people gathering on the edge of the dance floor. Still staggering, Abdul weaved his way through them, and moved toward a couple that was hug-ged together in the corner. Then he almost stumbled to the floor.

"Watch where you are going," the guy yelled, as Abdul nearly stumbled into them. Abdul mumbled that he was sorry and continued moving about unsteadily. Then he saw two girls from his English class. He moved over to ask the one named Teesha for a dance. Teesha was wearing her hair in braids, and her small chocolate face reflected surprise.

Abdul grabbed her hand and they headed toward the dance floor. On the floor, he moved about comically, making funny facial expressions and clowning. Quickly he tired out, thanked Teesha, with a slur, and headed, swaggering, back to his table. Then he started looking for Diane. His eyes searched the dance floor. Then he stumbled from table to table, unable to find her. Finally, he returned to his table and fell into his seat. He didn't see Bo, who was observing him from a distance, and was starting over in the direction of Abdul's table.

"Man, do you look a mess," Bo said, looking at Abdul with disgust. Abdul just sat there, his head hung down, mumbling to himself. Bo looked around the room. Then Abdul felt Bo take him by the elbow. Before long, he was in the restroom, bent over a sink. Bo was splashing water in his face. By then, it was very late. The noise from the dance floor outside was quieting and the people could be heard leaving.

Soon Bo and Abdul left the dance. Bo drove Abdul's car. They stopped at an all-night cafe. A brunette wearing a white uniform walked over and filled their cups with steaming hot coffee. "May I take your order please," she smiled warmly.

"No thanks. Coffee is all." Bo said, returning her smile. She wrote a receipt and sat it on the counter. "Thank you," she said softly, walking away. Bo put the cup down and turned to face Abdul.

"How you feeling, Abdul," he asked.

"Better," Abdul said dryly, looking up at Bo.

"Let me tell you something about drinking," Bo said.

"Look, man," Abdul cut in, "I don't want to hear it. I messed up—Okay."

"I'm not getting on your case," Bo said. " I just want to tell you a story my Pop once told me. It's about the grape."

Bo signalled for the waitress to bring more coffee. She walked over and refilled the cups, smiling warmly. When she finished, Bo continued, "long, long ago, before the flood, the grape was so weak in content, it couldn't produce a strong enough wine. So after the flood, God told Noah that he must take the blood from a lion, a pig, and a monkey to fertilize the grapevine."

Bo paused and sipped his coffee. "This was to make the grape stronger. As you can see, the grape has become very strong. When a person takes his/her first drink, s/he becomes bold, like a lion. After a few more drinks, s/he starts acting silly like a monkey. After a few more and s/he starts getting sloppy like a pig." He stopped and looked at Abdul straight in the eyes. They stared at each other for a few seconds and Abdul started grinning. Then they both laughed.

"Okay—I get the message," Abdul said. "Thanks for everything. Oh—by the way, did Diane get home okay?"

Bo looked at him sympathetically. "Yeah man, she made it home all right."

"I guess I blew it with her—didn't I?" Abdul asked. Bo just looked at him in silence. He didn't want to tell him that she'd left the dance with Slim, and that it had nothing to do with Abdul being drunk.

Chapter Four

When Abdul woke up the next morning, his head felt as though it was going to split open. It was the first hangover he'd ever experienced. He got out of bed and looked into the mirror. He could hardly recognize the face peering back at him. His eyes were bloodshot and dark bags were under his eyes. He looked like he had aged ten years.

He usually went to church with his mother on Sunday mornings, but he knew he wouldn't make it this morning. He told his mother that he had a stomach ache. His mother and Sonny went to church without him. Remaining in his bed, he reviewed the events of the previous night.

"Everything went just fine until I drank the Scotch," he reasoned. "I handled the reefer okay, but I shouldn't have mixed the two. No—I shouldn't even have smoked the reefer. Like Bo said, that stuff will mess you up." He wondered how Diane got home, but dismissed the thought as his headache worsened. His head was throbbing and his stomach felt nauseated. The pain was becoming unbearable. He rushed to the bathroom to throw up.

"Uuuuh—Uuuhh," he gulped, bending over the toilet.

When he finished throwing up, he looked inside the medicine cabinet for some aspirin. He swallowed several aspirins and drank a glass of water. Then he went into the kitchen to locate some stronger medicine. Suddenly the doorbell rang.

On the steps stood a short, slim, balding man wearing a business suit and carrying a suit case. He also carried a box of what looked like shoes.

"Are you Abdul Johnson," the man asked when Abdul opened the door.

"Yes," Abdul answered, puzzled.

"I believe you are on the Marshall High School basketball team. Is that not correct," he asked.

"Yes, I am," Abdul answered again, wondering what this

was all about.

"I represent Smart Shoe Manufacturing Company," the man explained. "I have a product in which you might be interested." Then the man went on to explain that he had attended several of the games in which Abdul had played, and that he thought that Abdul might be interested in a new product that was about to be released onto the market. This product, he explained, would greatly improve Abdul's performance on the court.

Abdul invited the man in, and, after gulping down two more aspirins, sat beside him on the couch. The man opened the shoe box he was carrying and showed Abdul a new pair of tennis shoes. The shoes had shiny red, black, and green labels on them that resembled Egyptian pyramids.

"I've got plenty of tennis shoes," Abdul commented, in disgust. "How can a tennis shoe, by itself, improve anyone's game?"

"You see, when you wear these shoes, you can do anything you want on the court. You can jump as high you want, make quick graceful moves to the basket, and shoot without missing."

"You mean I can do all of that?" Abdul asked, becoming somewhat more interested. He took one of the shoes in his hands and examined it more closely. The labels seemed to glow.

"We are looking for someone who will help to pilot test these shoes. You can have one pair at no charge, if you promise to wear them when you play. You will notice a difference. I will be watching and taking notes," the man added.

The man explained that, if the shoes were successful, they might soon be released onto the market and sold throughout the world.

"However, I must warn you of one thing," the man cautioned, looking Abdul straight in the eyes.

"What is that," Abdul said, thinking, "I knew there must be

a catch."

"If the labels come off, they will lose their powers. Do you understand?"

Abdul nodded, relieved, and took the shoes, thanking the gentleman and leading him to the door.

"All right then, they are yours—good luck," the man said, as he descended the front steps.

Eager to try out his new shoes, Abdul contemplated going to an old deserted school ground where nobody could see him. He waited for his mother to come home from church so that he could use her car. But he got impatient and decided to use his brother's bicycle. He put the tennis shoes in a tote bag, grabbed his basketball, and headed across town to the abandoned school. It took him about 40 minutes to reach the old deserted school yard.

When he arrived, he looked around carefully for signs of life, as his eyes passed over and the unkept grass, weeds, and boarded up windows. The sun shown brightly above, as clouds moved like ghosts against the blue sky. A slight November breeze stirred the ragged net hanging on the only remaining goal that stood above the aging concrete.

Abdul removed the tennis shoes from his bag, studied the label carefully, and slowly put them on. When he walked a few steps, he felt like he was walking on air. He picked up the basketball, bounced it a few times and took a shot at the basket. The ball when straight in. Each time he shot, the ball reached its target.

Hooks, jumpers, sets or impossible trick shots, the ball always went in—swish! Boy, did that sound good to his ears. He looked around once more to see if anyone was watching. Feeling assured that no one was looking, he took off toward the basket for a slam dunk. He became airborne from the middle of the court and glided all the way to the goal. When he reached the basket to stuff the ball, his head was three feet above the rim.

He warmed as the thrill of slamming the ball filled him with satisfaction. He spent another hour experimenting with the shoes, then headed for home. On the way he couldn't wait to tell Bo. But after thinking it over, he decided not to tell him.

"Some things you just got to keep to yourself," he reasoned. He also figured it best if he didn't show his skills all at once. He would improve a little at a time. That way people wouldn't suspect anything. They would assume he'd developed gradually, over time. When he went to bed that night, he slept well. The nightmares had gone away, no longer to haunt him.

Chapter Five

The steady patter of rain drops against Abdul's window woke him up. Monday morning had begun with a light shower. Through his window, he could see dark clouds gathering in the sky. It looked as if a rain storm was on its way. He jumped out of bed, feeling fresh and energetic. He picked up his designer tennis shoes and examined them once again. Then he put them in is tote bag. After dressing, he quickly put his room in order. Then he headed for school, too late to eat breakfast.

When he arrived at school, the first person he saw was Tina, walking toward her locker. He hurried to catch her. Tina looked at him and didn't say anything. Abdul walked beside her, trying to get her attention, but Tina kept walking, her nose high in the air.

"I'm sorry, Tina," Abdul said, trying to make up. "I was wrong for taking Diane to the dance." Tina gave him the evil eye and kept walking. After a few more attempts, Abdul gave up and headed for the gym.

It was during the afternoon practice that he first showed his newly acquired talents. He gained the attention he sought immediately. Scrimmage was in session between the first and second string. Abdul was guarding Slim, when Slim put a fake on him, making a quick move to the basket. When Slim reached the basket to dunk the ball, Abdul mysteriously recovered and blocked Slim's shot, rejecting the ball back into his face.

Abdul saw humiliation quickly cloud Slim's face, as he obviously tried to figure out how Abdul was able to block his shot. Abdul not only recovered from the move that Slim had made on him, but he jumped higher than Slim had expected.

After practice, Bo congratulated Abdul on his defense. "Man, that sure was a good block you put on Slim. I never saw you jump that high before." Bo said, watching Abdul untie his tennis shoes. "I see you got some new tennis, Abdul."

"Yeah, I got them over the weekend," Abdul responded, pretending to be indifferent.

"What kind are they," Bo asked, trying to get a closer look at the label.

"Just some cheap Nikes," Abdul lied, shoving his tennis shoes into his tote bag before Bo could read the label. He put the bag over his shoulder and headed towards the door. As he was leaving the gym, Coach Phillips stopped him and patted him on the back.

"That was an outstanding defensive play, Son," he said, as Abdul smiled and thought to himself, "You ain't seen nothing yet."

Several weeks passed by and Abdul began to slowly improve on the court, taking on a new appearance as a basketball player. Abdul's menacing defense was making it hard for Slim to get off a shot. When he did get a shot off, he had to work harder than ever.

He began to look confused and frustrated as he tried to make sense out of Abdul's sudden improvement. To make matters worse, Slim was becoming aware of Abdul's quick moves to the basket, his strong rebounding and his consistent jump shots. The coach also began to look at Abdul with renewed interest. In his entire coaching career, he had never seen a player improve so much so quickly. Abdul was playing so well that the coach decided to start him in the next game.

So one day after practice, the coach approached him. "Abdul, come here. I want to see you."

"Okay," Abdul said, walking to the side of the court.

The coach put his arms around Abdul's shoulders. "Abdul, you've been playing some real good ball lately. You have really proved your game. You've been playing consistently well on offense and defense."

He paused, looking at Abdul with admiration. Think you can handle a starting position?"

"Sure, Coach," Abdul said happily. "I can handle it."

Soon everyone was talking about Abdul. Students were stopping him to tell him what they'd heard. "I hear you're getting down in practice," one student said, as Abdul walked across campus.

"Yeah, a little." Abdul responded, shyly.

"I heard you made first string," said another.

"What about Slim? Did you play him out," asked another.

"No, the coach just moved him to the power-forward position," Abdul answered, surprised to hear what students were now thinking.

Later that evening, when Abdul's mother came home from work, he told her about his new starting position. "I will be starting in the game against Kennedy. That's the next game," he said, proudly.

"I'm happy to hear the good news, his mother said, smiling. "I'm so proud of you!" She hugged Abdul.

"They sure must be hurting for a center," Sonny laughed, shaking his head. "But at least I've got something to brag about."

Chapter Six

Marshall High's next game was with Kennedy High, one of the best teams in the city. The two teams had been rivals for years. Whenever they played, it was always a sell-out crowd. Kennedy High was in the affluent Green Haven area of the city. Because the residents of Green Haven had ample resources, they were able to get well-trained athletes. One of these athletes was Ray Hawkins, nick-named the 'Hawk' because of his leaping ability.

Hawk was a smooth basketball handler with slick moves to the basket. People compared his style with Gervin (Ice Man). "Hawk" could play guard or forward, and his coach used him at both positions, swinging him back and forth whenever necessary.

Last year "Hawk" scored 39 points in the game against Marshall, but Kennedy lost 99 to 101. Both teams had the same score during the last three seconds of the game when Slim hit a jumper at the buzzer. The basket won Marshall first place in the City Conference, and gave them a chance at the State Championship. Kennedy was eager to get revenge. Both teams were busy selling "wolf" tickets.

On the night of the game, Sacramento High's gym slowly filled with a capacity crowd. The air was thick with excitement and anticipation. From the doorway to the court, Abdul could see cheerleaders arousing an already intense crowd with yells of victory.

"Hey! Hey! What do you say? Whose gonna win the game today? We are! We are! Yea-a-a," they screamed.

"When the players entered onto the floor, the crowd yelled even louder. They even got a standing ovation. Loud shouts and cheers filled the gymnasium. When Slim ran out, several fans yelled, "Take it Slim, Baby!"

When Hawk ran out, several yelled, "What ya gonna do, big Hawk!" The crowd continued to roar as Abdul watched. During the pre-game warm-up, Slim and Hawk competed to please the crowd. One after the other made impressive slam dunks, but their slams looked amateurish compared to Abdul's. Abdul surprised everyone with a 360. He took off from the top of the key, made a full turn in mid air, and slammed the ball through the hoop with authority. Electrified, the crowd shouted into the air. The stunned fans roared with excitement.

"I ain't never seen nothing like that," shouted one fan.

"Who is he," asked a bald-headed stockily built man, sitting in the stands.

"Abdul Johnson," answered another man, sitting beside him.

"Where has he been all of this time," the stocky man asked.

"Warming the benches, I guess," the other man said.

The buzzer rang indicating two minutes before the game. Both teams huddled around their respective coaches. Abdul could hear Coach Phillips' husky voice bellowing out over the noise of the crowd.

"Okay, team, we've got to play like we want this one. They'll be out to get us. Play pressure defense. Keep a hand in the shooter's face; block, jump, and crash the boards! We've got to beat them on the boards to win the game. We want plenty of movement on offense to take good high percentage shots. Fill the lanes on the fast break and hustle back on 'D".

Slim, you'll be guarding Hawkins, so deny him the ball as much as possible."

He looked at Abdul "Son, there's a lot of responsibility riding on you playing center—so do your best." For a second, images of his dream, and the grinning specter of Slim, flashed across Abdul's mind, as he thought about the coach's words. "This is not a dream," he thought. "Tonight, I'm going to be a star—live and in color."

The game began with Hawk pumping in several quick jumpers from the perimeter and Slim countering with jumpers at the other end. Abdul scored often at low-post and high-post.

He also hit many jumpers from way out, and he avoided his man, making fancy moves to the basket, for slam dunks.

When he did, he seemed to glide in the air forever, as his long body twisted, turned and jerked to avoid the defensive maneuvers of his opponents. The crowd watched with fascination and disbelief. Abdul moved up and down the court like an alien from outer space, snatching rebounds, blocking shots, slam dunking, and throwing unbelievable passes.

At half time, in the locker room, Kennedy's coach anxiously tried to devise a strategy that could stop Abdul. "You guys are letting this game slip away," he yelled, scratching his head and looking at his players. It was obvious that the coach didn't understand how Marshall's team could be playing such good ball, or why they could not stop Abdul.

Anxiously, the coach tried to recall Abdul's name, looking frantically at the statistic's sheet. when he finally found his name, he couldn't recall anything about "this Johnson kid" from his scouting. He only remembered that Abdul usually didn't play that much."

"Okay fellahs," he finally told his team, "We'll have to start double-teaming, and if necessary, triple-teaming this Johnson kid."

"Where did he come from, Coach," one player asked.

"The way he's playing I'd say he came straight from hell." the coach answered, seemingly in a daze. "But we're not concerned about where he came from. We've got enough troubles trying to figure out how to stop him."

He looked down at his notes. "I want you guys to use the zone press and deny him the ball as much as possible." He put down his clip board and looked directly at Hawkins. "I want you to start posting down low."

"All right coach," Hawkins said.

When the second half began, Kennedy tried to make a run at Marshall High, using the fast break and pressure defense. They were successful at first, running off ten unanswered points, causing numerous turnovers with the zone press. Their traps appeared to have silenced Abdul, but part of the way through the second half, Abdul avoided their traps and broke the zone presses with incredible moves.

They double-teamed him, triple-teamed him, and at times the entire team tried to guard him, but he still somehow got the ball off for two points. Several times when Hawk drove past Slim for a basket, Abdul left the man he was guarding and rejected Hawk's shot.

Marshall won the game 128 to 115. It was not an easy victory. Hawk had a very good night, hitting 35 points and snatching 20 rebounds. Abdul, however, had 55 points, 12 block shots and 29 rebounds. In the sports column the next day, the Sacramento Bee wrote:

"Last night's contest was one of the most exciting high school games ever played. Both Slim and Hawk must be duly praised, but Abdul was magnificent! He was like the Michael Jordan or the Dr. "J" of high school basketball."

Another sports writer said, "Abdul Johnson is the best player to ever come out of high school."

Chapter Seven

From that night onward, things were never the same for Abdul Johnson. He'd become an instant hero, and stardom flooded his life like a tidal wave. When he was at school, people crowded around him, shaking his hand, and getting his autograph. They wanted to be near a celebrity. Slim was unhappy with the sudden change of events. He had to submit to playing second fiddle to Abdul. He was bewildered by Abdul's high level of performance. Abdul was now the "cock-of-the-walk".

He strutted around like a proud rooster, often with females on each arm. During the next two weeks Abdul continued to dominate and amaze on-lookers with his remarkable talents. He had improvising moves that were unknown to basketball. Whenever he played, whether at practice or in a game, people flocked to see him perform.

Soon scouts began to visit his games, from colleges throughout the country. National Basketball Association (NBA) scouts even came to watch him play. Once, during a half time, he noticed Bo motioning to a man sitting in the audience. The man had a round, friendly face and wore a beard. His sharp, deeply-set eyes peered from behind his thick eye-brows, as he studied the players.

Later, Abdul asked Bo who this man was. The man's face looked familiar to Abdul but he couldn't remember who he was.

"That's Red, from the Celts," said Jim, one of the other players.

"You mean Red Auerbach," Abdul asked, cutting his eyes in the man's direction.

"Yep, Red Auerbach," Jim said, and before he got the words out, Abdul took off and did a 360, slamming the ball with so much authority it caused the back board to vibrate.

Later that evening, after dinner, Abdul was doing his homework, when his mother sat beside him and said, "Son,

I got a call at work today from your coach."

Abdul put his pencil down and closed his book. He looked at his mother questionably, wondering why the coach would be calling his mother. His grades had improved. Could it be the coach somehow found out about the label on his tennis shoes? His mother's next words eased his mind.

"Sports Illustrated wants to do a feature story on you," she said, with excitement.

"Will I be in it too, Mama?" Sonny asked, breaking away from television.

"Maybe so. We'll have to wait and see," his mother answered. She looked at Abdul, who had a big smile on his face, and was deep in thought. "I'm so proud of you, Son."

Abdul just sat there in silence, imagining himself pictured in the magazine.

A week later, a team of reporters visited Abdul's home, interviewing and snapping pictures. They took several pictures of Abdul sitting on the sofa with his mother and Sonny. The grin on Sonny's face was brighter than the flash from the cameras. Afterwards, they visited his school, shooting pictures of Abdul strolling on campus, talking to other students.

Then they shot pictures of Abdul inside the gym playing basketball. When the magazine came out a week later, Abdul was on the cover poised for a slam dunk. When Tina saw Abdul's picture on the cover of Sport's Illustrated, her heart leaped with excitement. She bought several copies and showed them to her mother and cousins.

Since Abdul's rise to fame, he didn't have much time for Tina. He had to admit that he hardly notice her. Now he had his choice of all the girls. "I've got to make up for lost time," he thought.

One day, as he was walking through the hallway, he saw Miss Thompson, leaving the gymnasium. Miss Thompson smiled, as Abdul approached. "I am so proud of you," she said. "I knew you could do it."

She invited him into her office, and told him that she had something for him. As he entered her office, his eyes fell on a huge hard-bound book with the title, "Great African American Sports Heroes". The book had information about both ancient an modern Black sports figures. As he thumbed through the photographs and artist's sketches, he was amazed to learn that there were great Black athletes in Ancient Egypt and in Rome. He was happy to see pictures of some of the African American sports figures whose names he had heard so often, but had never seen. The book even contained pictures of all of the famous Olympic medal winners.

Miss Thompson told him that he could borrow the book and return it when he had time. She felt that it was important for him to know that his accomplishments were a part of a long tradition of excellence in the Black community.

That evening, Abdul showed the book to his mother and to Sonny. They were so proud of Abdul. Abdul would soon take his special place among famous African American athletes, they thought.

Chapter Eight

Colleges throughout the country began to send Abdul letters offering him scholarships. He received free trips to visit their campuses, and on weekends he traveled all across the country. One weekend he went to Texas. Then he went to Oklahoma, to North Carolina, and to New York.

When he was on planes stewardesses gave him special attention. He felt as though he was royalty. Everywhere he went, children stopped him to get his autograph. When he visited U.C.L.A., the college coach took him to a game where the Lakers were playing the Bulls. The UCLA coach invited Abdul to a public relations ceremony that would take place at half-time. There, Abdul met Magic Johnson and Michael Jordan.

At half-time, Abdul noticed television cameras focusing on him, as he stood beside Magic Johnson and then beside Michael Jordan. A commentator, with a pair of earphones on his head, held a microphone, and looked into the television camera to introduce the players. Then Abdul turned to face Magic Johnson.

"Magic, when most people hear the name Johnson, regarding basketball, they think of you. However, now we have another Johnson on the scene. What do you have to say about that," he asked, pointing the microphone at Magic Johnson.

"Well, Abdul Johnson is good. He's very good! He's got all of the right stuff to be a great player. He's got the height, the moves, and the creativity." He paused and looked at Abdul.

"But we all know there is only one Magic Johnson," he concluded.

"Jordan, I know you have got something to say about that," the commentator kept pushing.

"I have watched Abdul play," Jordan began. "He's got some special moves. He's got more hang time than I do," said Jordan. "We will have to wait and see."

"Well, Abdul, you don't mind if I call you A.J., do you," the commentator said.

"Fine with me," Abdul said, shyly.

"If you got an offer right now to play in the NBA, would you play," the commentator asked.

Abdul looked at Magic and then back to the microphone pointing at him. He spoke in a low voice, "That's hard to say right now. As it stands, I have to give serious attention to my education."

The commentator smiled. "What ever you decide, A.J., I'm sure we'll be seeing a lot of you in the future."

A week later, when Abdul returned home from his trip, his telephone rang repeatedly. People from everywhere were calling to say that they saw him on television. One evening, Bo came over, anxious for Abdul to tell him about his trip.

Man, you should have been there. I got a chance to meet Magic Johnson and Michael Jordan," he began.

"You did," Bo asked, startled. "What did they say to you?"

"Well, Jordan said that if I keep playing the way I am, I could definitely play in the NBA," Abdul fabricated, a little. He noticed the admiration in Bo's eyes.

"What about Magic," Bo continued. "What did he say?"

"Magic said I can bring more magic to the league," Abdul again fabricated, poking out his chest.

"There's no question about that!" Bo replied, brushing his hair.

By the end of the year, Marshall High School had won the City Conference. Abdul led the team to victory after victory. Now they faced the battle that would decide which school would be state champions.

Last year, Marshall had won the state championship and Coach Phillips had high hopes of winning again. The coach began working his players immediately. With Abdul playing such good ball, the coach reasoned that their chances of winning were great. Whenever it appeared that Abdul had reached his fullest potential, he'd surprise the coach with yet another dimension.

Abdul even inspired Bo to improve. Bo's shooting and ball-handling had improved considerably by the time of the state game. More importantly, Bo had taken a leadership role on the court. He had a new air of confidence. Abdul suspected that the coach was thinking that Bo could be his point guard next year.

One day, Abdul's mother came home with some startling news. Apparently, the owner of Sports Promotions, Inc. had contacted her boss about Abdul doing some commericals. Abdul's mother had been talking proudly about Abdul to her co-workers. One day Mr. Greenlee called her into his private office. She brought her pencil and paper, expecting to take dictation.

Her boss began right away. "I hear your son is playing excellent basketball," he had said, in a court-room trained voice. As she was about to answer, he continued.

"By the way, you won't need that," he nodded toward the tablet in her lap. "I have a contract for you to sign."

"A contract," she asked. "What kind of a contract?"

"Your son has a chance to make some money," he said, getting up and walking toward her with a document in his hand. "The owner of Sport's Promotions, Inc., is a close friend of mine. During lunch the other day, your son's name came up for a commercial spot. When he found out you worked for me, it clinched the deal."

Before long, Abdul began to make commercials. He was accustomed to being behind television cameras by now, but when he began shooting scenes for commercials, it was much more complicated, because acting became involved. However, after his initial stage fright passed, he did all right and enjoyed every moment of it.

The company shot his first commercial on the court of a neighborhood park. Abdul played basketball with a professional actor. In the commercial, he promoted a popular soft drink. For the next commerical, the company filmed the two of them on a bench talking and drinking the soda. The commercial became popular across the country. Abdul became as well-known as Magic Johnson and Michael Jordan.

He earned so much money from the commercials that he could purchase his mother a new living room set. It was something she had wanted for a long time. Then he surprised Sonny with a VCR machine and dozens of video tapes. Finally, he decided to purchase himself a car. Bo went with him to select the car. They traveled from one car dealer to another. Abdul almost bought an IROC Z, but, after much coaxing from Bo, decided to purchase a Corvette.

Abdul happily drove the shiny red Corvette off the lot.

Chapter Nine

Gradually Abdul's quiet, reserved manner became flamboyant. It was obvious that he enjoyed being a star. Like his friend Bo, he began to dress in expensive slacks and sweaters. He could be seen driving through town in his Corvette, with his shirt open and a gold chain around his neck. The gold chain matched his expensive gold watch.

Abdul was excited because Marshall High's team would soon travel to San Francisco for the state championship game. Leading up to the game, Abdul's face appeared regularly on television, and in newspapers, smiling and talking proudly while sports writers interviewed him for the upcoming tournament. High schools from all over California would be traveling to San Francisco for the game.

It would be shown on television during prime time. On campus one afternoon, Abdul and Bo were sitting in the cafeteria discussing the school dance and the game that would follow it. At the dance, they would select a Homecoming Queen. So far, there were three contestants.

"Abdul, do you know who the contestants are," Bo asked.

"Not really," Abdul replied in an unconcerned tone. "I haven't been keeping up with it." As an after thought, he said, "Probably Sonia."

"Yeah, she's one, but guess who else is," Bo replied.

"Who," Abdul asked.

"Well, there is a cute little blond in your English class. I think her name is Elizabeth," he said.

"Who else," Abdul asked.

"Tina," Bo answered, stroking his hair with his small brush.

"Tina," Abdul shouted, his eyes staring at Bo. "Man, you got to be kidding. How can Tina be running for Homecoming Queen, wearing those bifocals? She's too homely, man," Abdul continued, shaking his head.

"Oh, you haven't seen her lately," Bo asked.

After thinking for a minute, Abdul said, "I saw her a while

back and she looked the same to me."

"Well, my man, you are in for a big surprise," Bo laughed.

On the night of the dance, Abdul parked his slick red Corvette in the parking lot and walked jubilantly with Bo into Marshall's gym. The night air was clear and brisk, and Abdul's eyes were shining as bright as the moon outside.

As they walked into the gym, the first record was playing. It was from a Rhythm and Blues album. Abdul walked to the rear of the gym to take it all in. A slender young man, resembling Michael Jackson, moved gracefully on stage, blaring out popular lyrics. People where piling into the gym. It was obvious that everyone was having a good time. An hour later the band stopped playing and M.C. Michael Jackson look-a-like began talking over the microphone.

"Well, you all know what tomorrow is," he said with a high pitched voice.

"Yeah," the crowd echoed back, almost in unison.

"I hope you all can be there to support the team. Several buses are leaving for San Francisco tomorrow at noon." he paused and signaled for the cheerleaders, standing by the stage. The cheerleaders broke out in their most popular routine. Then the Michael Jackson look-a-like called the Principal, Coach Phillips and the entire basketball to the stage.

They all huddled around on the stage while the principal and Coach Phillips gave a speech then each player waved his hand. When Abdul raised his hand, the crowd clapped and roared for an exceptionally long time.

When everyone left the stage, the M.C. continued, "Next I'm happy to have the pleasure of introducing one of our most distinguished teachers, Miss Monique Thompson. Miss Thompson will, in turn, introduce the three outstanding young ladies who are competing to become Homecoming Queen.

Miss Thompson walked onto the stage. She wore a classy blue silk dress that went well with her skin color. She had a very sophistocated demeanor. She was a good role model for the young women at the dance.

"Thank you," she said, speaking softly into the microphone. "Tonight we're going to select the Homecoming Queen for the class of '90. We have three beautiful contestants."

She began introducing them one at a time. She was careful to make positive and encouraging coments about each contestant.

"She really cares about her students," thought Abdul. "What a gentle and sincere person she is."

As each contestant walked onto the stage, she presented the contestant with the same question. She explained that each contestant had only three minutes to answer the question.

Sonia was the first contestant to be called. She was wearing an elegant red dress. She walked across the stage with an air of confidence. Miss Thompson greeted her warmly and then asked the question, "What is the greatest challenge facing young people today?"

Sonia smiled brightly. "I speak from the perspective of an African American high school student," she began. "The most serious challenge facing African American students today is making an impact on the course of African American history, and on American history in general. We must continue the long and proud tradition of our ancestors. We must carry the race proudly into the 21st Century."

At first the audience seemed stunned at the seriousness of the response. Then suddenly, the audience broke into an applause which continued for nearly 30 seconds.

Miss Thompson thanked her and then introduced Elizabeth Atkins, a petite intelligent girl with long, blond hair. Her blue eyes matched her blue satin dress. Miss Thompson asked Elizabeth the same question.

Elizabeth took a deep breath, and answered confidently. "I speak as a young American woman, living during the decade of the 1990s. In my opinion, the most critical issue facing young women today is gaining equal rights. I believe that women should fight to get equal pay for equal work, and that they should struggle for equal protection under the law. We must elevate the status of American womanhood. This must be our top priority."

The audience again applauded thunderously, showing approval that the women who would represent their school were intelligent as well as beautiful.

Finally, Miss Thompson called Tina to the stage. Abdul watched Tina's queenly figure as she moved gracefully to the center of the stage. She moved very quickly, almost like an African bird. He couldn't believe what he saw. Tina was no longer wearing her glasses. "She must be wearing contact lenses," he thought. "She looks so different."

She wore a long dress with a sequenced design at the shoulders. The sequins caused her already sparkling eyes to seem larger than Abdul had ever seen them. Her long braids had pearls and baby's breath flowers embedded in them, giving her an angelic glow. When Miss Thompson read her the question, her bright smile lit up the stage.

However, today, her braces were gone. Bo was standing next to Abdul, smiling. "I said you would be surprised, didn't I," he said.

Abdul continued to stare at Tina.

"The most critical issue facing young people today is survival," she began. "Collectively, we must stop acting in ways that will result in our destruction. We must stop taking drugs. We must stop becoming parents too soon, and we must stop dropping out of school. We need to educate ourselves for future leadership, so that, when our day comes, we will be able to help those young people who will follow in our footsteps."

Next was the talent contest. Sonia sang a song once peformed by Roberta Flack. Then Elizabeth did a comedy routine resembling a monologue of Joan Rivers. However,

Tina stole the show. Wearing black leotards, she performed a modern dance to a cut from a Wynton Marsalis album.

After the talent contest, the judges went out of the room while the crowd danced. When the judges returned, they announced Tina as the winner. She had won by a unanimous vote. After the crowd applauded, the crowd began to dance again. Abdul kept trying to get a dance with Tina, but she was always busy dancing with someone else. When the dance was over, she left before he was able to talk to her.

Later that night, while attempting to fall asleep, Abdul tried to think about the state championship game, and the next day's team practice, but images of Tina kept entering his mind. "How could I have been so blind," he thought. "I have known her all of these years and I never realized how beautiful, intelligent, and sexy she is."

He looked down at his tennis shoes with the designer label again. Then tired, and frustrated, he finally fell asleep.

Chapter Ten

The next morning Abdul woke up earlier than usual, excited about today's game. Within minutes, he had taken a shower and had put on a new sweater, a new pair of pants, and a new gold chain. Quickly he stuffed his tennis shoes into his tote bag, and examined the labels again to be sure that they were still there.

As he descended the stairs, heading for the kitchen, he noticed that his mother and Sonny were already dressed and were eating breakfast. On the couch in the living room, he could see that their luggage was already packed and ready to be put in the family car. His mother and Sonny would leave for the game shortly after Abdul left with his teammates.

Abdul ate with classic speed this morning, and then darted out the door, jogging toward Marshall High School. He wanted to be sure that he didn't miss the bus that would take the team to San Francisco.

When Abdul ran into the locker room, it was busy with activity. Lockers were slamming open and shut, and teammates were stuffing their luggage with everything they needed for the game. Abdul stopped suddenly at the bench that stood in front of his locker. He took his tennis shoes from his tote bag and placed them on the bench, planning to untie his regular shoes and put on the tennis shoes.

After he had taken his shoes off, he arose to put them in his locker. His eyes fell on the door of his locker. He was shocked! On the front of his locker was a picture of him with lipstick painted on his lips, a woman's earring in his ears and a long skirt covering his pants. A dart was pointing at his forehead.

As he stood there, he could hear Slim's voice from behind the adjacent row of lockers, poking fun at Abdul.

"He's not man enough for Tina," he laughed. "Didn't you see him last night? He couldn't even get a dance with her. She wants a real man, like me. Abdul is nothing but a sissy!"

"Get out of my business, man," Abdul shouted from the other side of the lockers. "I've told you a thousand times to stay out of my business."

"Look at him," Slim laughed, with jealousy in his eyes. "He whines just like a girl! What would Tina want with him?"

This was too much for Abdul. Instantly, his fist went toward Slim's chin. Slim darted out of the way, but Abdul kept coming for him. It required several teammates to hold Abdul down, and several more to hold Slim down, who was soon throwing punches back at Abdul. They both landed on top of the bench and the designer shoes. Suddenly Coach Phillips entered the locker room and yelled, "Quit horsing around! Are you crazy? We've got less than fifteen minutes to board the bus! The Homecoming Queen, her court and the cheerleaders are already on the bus, waiting for you. Let's get a move on it, before we're late!"

Still angry, Abdul tore the picture away from his locker, crumbled it up and threw it in the wastebasket near the door. Then he went back to put on his tennis shoes.

Again, Abdul was startled. His eyes fell on the tennis shoes in disbelief. The labels were gone! Frantically, he looked under the bench. The labels were not there. He looked inside of the tennis shoes. They were not there. Then he darted over to the wastebasket. He opened the picture that he had just crumbled. The label was not there. He opened his tote bag and dumped everything out onto the bench. Then he combed through everything over and over again. The labels were not there either.

By then, most of the teammates had already boarded the bus. Anxiety set in as he was caught between the possibility of the team leaving without him, and of his leaving without the labels on his tennis shoes. "Without the labels, I won't be able to lead Marshall High to victory ever again", he thought.

Suddenly Coach Phillips stormed into the locker room. "Abdul, what is wrong with you today? You're holding up the

team. We almost left you! Let's get a move on it!"

Abdul could see the headlights on the bus outside, and could hear the motor beginning to start. Everyone was waiting for him. With no other choice, he quickly put on the tennis shoes, grabbed his tote bag and ran for the bus.

"Where could they be," Abdul thought, as he ran across the parking lot. "Did someone steal them?"

Abdul found a seat at the back of the bus. Tina had saved a seat for him beside her. She smiled as he put his tote bag in the compartment above their seat and sat beside her.

"I can't tell her what happened," he said, forcing a smile at Tina. "I can't tell anyone!"

Abdul slumped into his seat feeling dejected. He was deep in thought. He didn't feel like talking to Tina. He was too busy trying to figure a way out of his predicament.

He thought about how everyone would be watching him play tonight—his friends, his fans, his coach and the nation! "Without the labels on those shoes, I will be a nobody again," he thought.

"What's wrong, Abdul," Tina's voice suddenly broke into Abdul's thoughts. "Are you sick or something? Why are you so quiet?"

"Oh, I meant to tell you, congratulations. I wanted to get a dance with you last night, but you were too occupied," he tried to joke.

Soon, his attention was distracted again. An idea formed in his head. I'll pretend that I'm sick!" Then he began to think about different illnesses that he could fake.

"I'll tell the coach that I sprang my ankle. No, they might check that out," he thought, frantically. Then he looked out the window into space, staring at the countryside as it raced past. He tried to think of another angle.

"What about the flu," he asked himself. "No, they can check that one out too." After considering a myriad of other possibilities, from a bad back to diarrhea, he dropped the idea of lying his way out of the game, and tried to think of something else.

He pushed the button beside his seat causing his seat to tilt backwards in a reclining position. Then he closed his eyes, and tried to use his imagination. He toyed with the idea of running away. He went over all of the places that he might go—Los Angeles, Cuba, Africa.

"No, I might be able to get the money, but I can't leave my mother and Sonny way out here in San Francisco looking for me," he concluded. "Oh well, I might as well face the music."

"Fame and fortune were good while they lasted," he thought.

He stared at the countryside as it raced past. Then, somewhat depressed, he fell asleep.

Chapter Eleven

The San Francisco fog hung over the Cow Palace like a fine mist, increasing the chill of the cold night air. From the window of the bus, Abdul could see the yellow buses dotting the parking lot, along with an array of different colors of cars. Scalpers were hustling tickets outside, and television crews were moving their equipment into the huge arena. Thousands of fans were lined up, anxious to fill the empty seats.

Inside the locker room players chatted excitedly while changing into their game uniforms. Bo was watching Abdul with curiosity. "You all right Abdul? You don't look to swell today."

Abdul slammed his locker shut, stood up and gave Bo an annoyed look. "Don't worry about me. I'm doing just fine," Abdul snapped. Then he walked away, ignoring Bo, even though he realized that Bo was watching him.

It was obvious that Bo was wondering what was wrong with Abdul.

Another game was already in session so they had to wait until it was over. While they were waiting, the Marshall High School team assembled on the front row, and watched the game. Abdul's eyes traveled slowly over what looked like a sea of human faces. He bit down on his lower lip. Then he looked down at the tennis shoes he was wearing. He wished that they still had power.

His mother and Sonny were sitting a few rows above him, looking down at him with love and admiration. He tried to flash a quick smile. His eye caught a heavy set man, sitting near his mother, with his face flushed from drinking too much beer before the game. The man pointed at him and said, "Isn't that the Johnson kid?"

Before the man's companion could reply, Sonny interrupted and said, "Yeah, that's him. He's my brother. That's Abdul." Sonny continued to shove more popcorn into his face, with his face beaming with pride. The first game ended, and the Marshall Bears began to move onto the floor.

At the opposite end, Fremont from Los Angeles, began going through their warm-ups. Occasionally a player would slam dunk and glance toward the players at the other end. People were watching Abdul. They wanted to see one of his famous slam dunks. However, it didn't happen.

When Abdul got to the basket, he just laid up the ball. Sonny leaned over and whispered to his mother. "How come Abdul's not slamming the ball, Mama?"

A worried expression clouded her face, but she managed a smile. "He probably just doesn't want to show off right now," she said.

When the two minute warning sounded, the players gathered around Coach Phillips as he went over usual last minute instructions. He glanced at Abdul. "You all right, Abdul?"

"I'm fine, Coach," he said, trying to avoid the coach's glare. The game began at a fast pace, with both teams scoring several quick baskets. Then Fremont gradually took the lead and Coach Phillips called time out to change the momentum of the game.

"Okay team," he said in the huddle. "They are trapping and denying Abdul the ball! Set more screens and picks, take advantage of the over play by using the back door." He looked at Abdul.

Abdul could see that he was wondering why he was having such a hard time evading the other team's traps. In the past, it had been impossible for any team to contain Abdul. Abdul knew the Coach was thinking that the problem was Fremont's tenacious defense. "He has no idea that the problem has to do with the missing labels," he thought, feeling sorry for himself.

Abdul remained silent on offense. The man he was guarding took Abdul inside for slams and consistently hit perimeter jumpers. The crowd was booing. Probably the most disgusted were those who had come from as far away as New York just to see Abdul play.

Instead of seeing a superstar, they were seeing what they considered a mediocre player who couldn't even hold the ball. Abdul made no spectacular moves to the basket. He made no block shots. He made no magnificent slams. Soon, Abdul could hear the crowd shouting nasty comments from the stands.

He could hear the heavy set man who drank too much beer yelling to Sonny, "Hey! What's wrong with your brother? He can't make a basket!" He knew that Sonny was melting into his seat. It was so painful for Abdul to hear the man laughing at him, in front of his brother.

Finally the coach substituted him. Marshall trailed 46 to 52 at half time.

At half-time, Abdul was surprised to see Tina, walking toward him on the bench. She had asked the coach for special permission to talk to Abdul during half-time, hoping that she could give him the encouragement he needed to turn his game around.

She stood near the end of the bench, and motioned toward him. Most of the teammates had gone back into the locker room, so Tina and Abdul were practically alone on the bench.

Something in Tina's smile let Abdul know that he could trust her. "Come on, now, Abdul," she began. "You know that I have stuck by you in thick and thin, bad weather and good weather. Tell me what is wrong?"

Swallowing hard, Abdul broke the news. He told her about the day when the shoe manufacturer came to his house with the tennis shoes and the designer labels. Then he told her how his game had improved so dramatically when he began playing in these shoes.

He told her about the fight in the locker room and about the missing labels. Swallowing hard again, Abdul told her how afraid he was, that he would be a nobody again.

"You have got to be kidding, Abdul," Tina said when he finished. "You'll never be a nobody! Your power is not in a silly tennis shoe label! It is within you!"

"Don't you see, she continued. "That man who sold you the shoes probably got them hot and just wanted to get rid of them. He had probably heard that you were on the basketball team, and he probably knew that most people would try anything to be a superstar."

"Abdul, it's not in the label. It is all in your mind. If you put as much confidence in yourself and in your God-given abilities, you can succeed! Remember, Abdul, God made you in his image, not tennis shoe labels! You've got the talent to succeed without the labels! I've watched you. I know!"

"You don't need the labels," she continued. "Think positively, Abdul! Go on back out there and give it your best. You can do it!" She reached for his hand.

Suddenly Abdul heard the buzzer signalling the beginning of the second half. He hugged Tina and then headed for the other end of the bench.

Marshall High was lagging behind Fremont. Coach Phillips was still using strategy after strategy to avoid defeat, and Slim seemed to be working overtime, trying to regain what was once his star position on the team. Soon there were only 8 minutes left in the game. Surprisingly enough, Coach Phillips put Abdul back in the game.

By then Abdul had had time to think about what Tina had said. A surge of confidence entered his being, as he remembered what Tina said about talents being God-given.

The crowd booed and the fans of the opposing team yelled with delight as Abdul entered the court again. By then, everyone had lost confidence in Abdul's ability to deliver.

The Marshall High School cheerleaders attempted to arouse the Marshall high school fans, with their favorite cheer.

"Hey! Hey! What do you say? Whose gonna win the game today? We are! We are! Yea-a-a," they screamed.

Then Fremont ran out, and the crowd yelled, "Take it Fremont! Take it!" Then the Marshall High School fans gave a sudden thunderous roar, as Abdul surprised everyone. He took off from the top of the key, and slammed the ball through the hoop with authority. It wasn't as fancy as before, but it counted the same.

"Do it, Abdul, a fan shouted.

"He's coming back," the man who drank too much beer shouted back at Sonny!

Sonny sat up straight grinning from ear to ear.

Then, seemingly out of nowhere, Fremont pumped several quick jumpers from the perimeter and Slim countered with jumpers at the other end. Abdul scored at the low and high-post. He avoided his man and made some fancy moves to the basket. He made several slam dunks.

He was successful in avoiding most of the defensive maneuvers of the opposing players. The crowd roared with approval.

The opposing team tried to make a run at Marshall high, using fast breaks and pressure defense, but they were not successful. Abdul avoided their traps and broke the zone presses.

First Marshall tied the game. Then Marshall soared past Fremont to take the state championship.

Chapter Twelve

The trip back to Marshall was a very happy one. The cheer-leaders, in the back of the bus, sang one cheer after another. Tina smiled and held Abdul's hand. "See, I knew that you could do it," she said.

The long bus ride provided time for Tina and Abdul to talk. They had missed talking to one another, now that both of them had become so busy. Tina started teasing Abdul about the designer labels, and she praised him about the wonderful talents that he found in himself alone. Abdul laughed, wondering how he could have been so silly.

Then Tina told him that he wasn't silly. She shared with him a similar experience that she had.

"Not too long ago, people thought I was ugly. I thought that I was ugly too. I thought that being beautiful had to do with whether a person wore glasses or whether a person wore braces. I also thought it had something to do with how light your skin was."

Abdul was quiet, feeling a little guilty because he had once thought of Tina in this way.

"I always looked on the outward appearance rather than in my own heart, to discover who I am," she continued.

"Then one day, I heard a minister talk about how important it is for Black people to believe in themselves, and in the God-given talent and beauty that they have," she continued. "He said that beauty comes from within."

"Once I believed this, I began to see myself in a different way. I began to see the beauty that was beneath my bifocals and braces. I began to act, walk, and think like a beautiful person. Soon others thought of me as a beautiful person, too."

"It wasn't in the bifocals or the braces. I could have taken them off and I would still have felt ugly," she continued. "It was only in discovering I am a beautiful African queen, I then learned how beautiful and talented I am," she said.

Abdul looked at her in amazement, remembering the night

of the Homecoming Queen pageant.

"You are beautiful, too.—Even if you never become a world- famous basketball star," she added.

Tears formed at the corners of his eyes as he began to talk. He told her all about the nightmares he used to have. He talked about his obsession with becoming a great basketball star and how easy it was for him to be fooled with the supposedly designer labels that had power.

He talked about how hurt he felt when the same fans who had cheered him at one time, turned on him as soon as he had a weak moment.

"You don't need to depend on what others think of you, Abdul," Tina said. "The power is in believing in yourself."

The bus stopped in front of Marshall High School. Soon Tina and Abdul walked, hand-in-hand from the bus, across the parking lot and into the school.

They could hear loud cheers from the gymnasium where the students had planned a special surprise reception for the players, the cheerleaders, and for the Homecoming Queen.

When Abdul walked in, the students cheered loudly and rushed him. Some of their younger brothers and sisters were waiting with pictures of Abdul, wanting him to autograph them. Sonny stood up in the bleachers, smiling from ear to ear. Abdul's mother stood nearby, proud of her son.

A local television sports commentator made his way toward Abdul with a camera crew. He pointed a microphone at Abdul, and asked, "Abdul you didn't play that well during the first half of the game. In fact, Coach Phillips actually took you out of the game. Then you made a dramatic comeback. What happened?"

Abdul smiled at Tina.

"I learned to believe in myself. There is power in believing in your God-given abilities. It you believe in the talents that God has given you, you can turn many bad situations around," Abdul said, confidently.

In the weeks that followed, Abdul got the opportunity to share his new insights with Bo, and with many other students at the school. He was able to tell them they had God-given abilities and they should believe in themselves.

He told his brother Sonny how important it was for him to discover the beautiful Black person that he is. Sonny was amazed. He thought Abdul believed he was only a child! It made him so happy to know that the brother he admired so much, thought so much of him.

He told his mother that she was a beautiful African American queen, and that he was proud to be her son. She was surprised that Abdul had become so serious in his outlook on life.

Sports commentators from throughout the state interviewed Abdul. However, in every interview, Abdul stressed the importance in believing in oneself and in having confidence in one's God given abilities. Sportswriters began talking about how Abdul seemed to have changed. Young people throughout the nation were inspired by him.

Soon basketball season was over and Abdul spent more time with his studies, strengthening his grade point average so that he wouldn't have any trouble playing on the team next year. Students throughout Marshall High School admired Abdul. It had been a very good year, and he had learned some of the most valuable lessons in his life.

ISBN 0-913543-15-2 $6.95

Do you like designer clothes and shoes?
Does the label make them better?
Who would you take to the big dance? Your best friend or
someone who looks good, but you barely know?
Are the odds better to become a rap or basketball star, or a
computer programmer or similar skilled profession?

Read Abdul and the Designer Tennis Shoes

Abdul and the Designer Tennis Shoes is an excellent book for
our youth. It's easy to read, entertaining, and raises significant
issues about values. William McDaniels has done a great job.

Jawanza Kunjufu
Author and Publisher